"I found My Possessive Bodyg
can't say enough how much I
were all so perfect. Nathan beir
want to read more and more. S
the feelings I got from reading
trusted each other and already committed themselves, before they
dating, is what I call trust. And these characters trusted each other with
their life on the line. Whether it be Nathan losing his job or being away
from Hannah or Hannah being kidnaped and tortured. Anyways, if you're
looking for a heartwarming, funny, and a steamy book, this one's for you."
-Annie Ferrer, *Goodreads*

"...I love romance and this surely knew how to make me feel emotions
and things I didn't even know I could feel. I had butterflies throughout the
book and the author was honestly, surprisingly very good at cliffhangers
and keeping us at suspense. My Possessive Bodyguard was a wonderful,
enthralling read that I have re-read over a dozen times because I can't get
enough of it..."
-Caterina Faye, *Goodreads*

"The plot in this is really good and keeps things exciting and thrilling. It
was one of the first books I read on Wattpad and I still like to re-read it
every now and then. I've also got my friends into the book and they loved
it!"
-Erei Sagato, *Goodreads*

"This is one of all-time favourite books and I'm sure I've read it more than
5 times already now. Nathan, the bodyguard is so dreamy and cutely
possessive that it melts my heart. I wish I could get a Nathan in real life.
Also Nathan's chemistry with Hannah is unbeatable. I love this book so
much; it's beautiful."
-Harbani Sachdeva

"This book will pull all your emotions out, as you continue to flip through
each page. There's no other book quite like this one, as you fall in love by
the first chapter and can't set the story down afterwards. I've re-read this
book three times, and every time I begin to read it, I can't stop reading it
until I sadly get to the end. Jamilexis Gallardo knows how to keep her
audience hanging and she does it well."
-Kyaira Mitchell

Typewriter Pub, an imprint of Blvnp Incorporated
A Nevada Corporation
1887 Whitney Mesa DR #2002
Henderson, NV 89014
www.typewriterpub.com/info@typewriterpub.com

ISBN: **978-1-68030-996-6**

DISCLAIMER
This book is a work of fiction. The characters, incidents, and dialogue are drawn from the author's imagination and are not to be construed as real. While references might be made to actual historical events or existing locations, the names, characters, places, and incidents are either products of the author's imagination or are used fictitiously, and any resemblance to actual persons living or dead, business establishments, events or locales is entirely coincidental.

MY POSSESSIVE BODYGUARD

JAMILEXIS GALLARDO

type
writer
pub

To my Wattpad readers

FREE DOWNLOAD

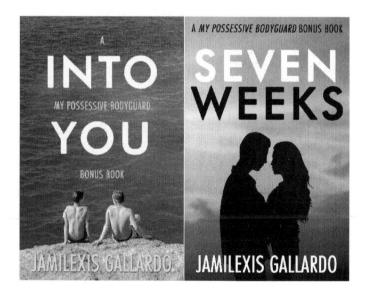

Get these freebies and more when you sign up for
the author's mailing list!

jamilexis-gallardo.awesomeauthors.org

CHAPTER 1

The freezing cold air hit me like a pile of bricks, sweeping my long brown hair all over my face. If it were any other girl, it would look like a shampoo commercial but I was pretty sure I just looked all dorky and stupid. I pulled my hair away, cringing when my icy cold fingers touched my cheeks.

This was exactly why I didn't like having my hair down, I hated having to take care of it. My hair was wavy but it was also frizzy and those two didn't make a good combination. I usually liked to put it up in a high ponytail but my hair kept me warm, and in this freezing New York weather, I constantly had to find ways to keep myself warm. I wasn't complaining; I loved this weather. I loved wearing cozy sweaters and scarfs and sitting close to the window somewhere with a hot cup of coffee.

I walked down the stairs as people rushed past me. I had just taken my last final of the semester and it sure felt great. Being a college student kept me really busy, but I didn't mind at all. I liked having something to do. Especially after going through the worst possible break-up ever...

Don't go there, Hannah.

"Ms. Collins," Robin, my bodyguard for the day, greeted me with a nod when I made it back to the car. All of my dad's bodyguards looked pretty much the same: tall, muscular, and always in black suits with white shirts and black ties. They also wore an earpiece so they could all be in communication in case something happened. Most people would drool over them and I probably would too, if they weren't with me *all the time.*

I didn't always have bodyguards.

1

My dad was a famous actor. He had been acting since he was a teenager but his big break-out movie came out about five years ago, making his popularity skyrocket. Around the same time, my mom was attacked in a restaurant parking lot. The men took her purse, jewelry, and her car but not before beating her. My dad's success had put a spotlight on my family and people now knew my family had a lot of money which put us in danger. So we moved to a house with much more security and my dad hired an army of bodyguards.

It wasn't just my dad's success that put us in danger. My oldest brother, Colton, was the owner of the most famous nightclub in New York. Nicholas, my second oldest brother, had started our family's clothing brand company and he ran it as the CEO. A year ago, my youngest brother had decided he wanted to pursue a modeling career. He was currently in Paris.

Who knew success came with a cost? It cost us our safety which was what the bodyguards were for.

Unlike my brothers, I had yet to start my career. I didn't have the same talent as Nick and Colton in running a business or the flawless looks to become a model like my brother Derek. I liked to draw.

I wanted to be a wedding gown designer. I loved designing dresses and had a lot of sketch books in my room where I had started drafting a lot of dresses. Some pages just had doodles, others had the silhouette of a dress; each page had a random design that only I understood. The problem was that I had yet to finish a single whole gown; I always just stopped in the middle of it and started a new one.

I got in the car and Robin shut the door. I watched as he went around it and got in the driver's seat. I looked out the window as he began to drive.

Good-bye school, I thought happily as I watched us pass by the school.

I loved school but finals week killed me mentally and drained me physically. It was enough to make me not want to set

2

eyes on school for a while. I had a whole month to myself. I could lie around in my room, not doing anything *and* not feel guilty about it. It was official: I had nothing to do but draw all day if I wanted...or sleep.

Robin pulled up into the driveway and I watched as he input the six-digit code so the gates could open.

My favorite part of the house was outdoors: the green grass, the big trees, and the different flowers planted in strategic places to make up the garden. The house was beautiful, of course, but I always thought it was too big. I never understood my dad's logic in moving us into a much bigger house after my mom's attack. I thought it made it easier for intruders to break in because there were more windows and more doors to break into. Of course, I knew that it was my vain mother who had a lot to do in choosing the house.

The car stopped in front of the house and I opened the door before Robin had time to reach it. "I got it." I smiled at him.

He nodded but hurried to open the front door for me. I couldn't help but roll my eyes at him. I could open my own doors, thank you very much. I wasn't the famous actress or rich businessman. I wished they wouldn't treat me like I was royalty when the only reason I needed bodyguards was because of my family's success. I was no one.

Inside, the house was warm and spotless clean, like always. The living room was the first thing you saw when you walked in, with very expensive and elegant furniture. Everything in the house was so expensive and beautiful and new. The furniture, the decorative ornaments, the expensive floor almost made this house feel like an exhibit rather than a home.

Money had cost me my parents. Especially my mom.

"Honey? Is that you?" my mom called as she hurriedly made her way into the living room. Her face fell when she saw that it was just me. My mom was a very attractive woman. She was tall with perfect hips and short blond hair with piercing blue eyes. I looked nothing like her. She was always dressed up, as if ready to meet the President of the United States. I often thought how exhausting it must be to be her but she seemed to love being Christina Collins, Richard Collins's first and only wife.

Today, she was wearing a pale pink pencil dress with white high heels, her hair was straight and she had perfect make up on. She did not look forty-five.

"Dad isn't home yet?" I asked taking off my jacket.

"He'll be here soon," she said looking annoyed by my comment.

My dad was supposed to be here last week. He was out, doing interviews or something. He was currently not working in any movie and was supposed to be here by now.

"Okay," I said as I began to make my way up the stairs.

"Dinner is almost ready," Mom called behind me.

I just nodded.

I didn't have the best relationship with my mom. It wasn't always like this but money and fame had really gotten to her. Ever since my dad became famous, she began to worry about appearances more than anything. She wasn't that motherly either, she only cared about looking good in front of the cameras. It was stupid, but I couldn't change that. She also cared more about her sons with big businesses and careers. I think she began to be even more distant with me when I refused to let her open a business to start my own brand. She didn't understand that I wanted to graduate first. She didn't understand the fact that I wasn't ready—I didn't even have a full gown finished! She found it stupid that I didn't want to be successful because of my dad, just like everyone else. I wanted to be successful on my own.

My phone began to ring just as I reached my room and I smiled when I looked at the caller ID.

"Hey, Pat," I answered taking off my scarf.

"Hannah Banana, how are you?" he said on the other end.

I used to cringe when he started calling me 'Hannah Banana' back in middle school but I began to get used to it when I realized he wasn't going to stop calling me that. Apparently, he thought he invented that nickname.

I smiled. "Good."

"What are you up to?"

"Nothing," I said as I closed my bedroom door.

"Oh come on, anything interesting? I didn't call you to be bored to death."

I laughed. "I'm done with finals?" I offered.

"Mmm... that's something I guess."

Patrick and I had been best friends since we were in middle school. He was truly my other half. I never thought a guy would understand me better than a girl but it was true. He understood me better than anyone. After we graduated from high school, he moved to Miami for school and I haven't seen him since then.

"What are you doing?" I asked throwing myself on the bed.

"Getting ready for the club, baby!" he yelled in my ear. "Hold up—I'm going to FaceTime you because I need outfit advice."

"Okay," I said rolling my eyes. He hung up and FaceTimed me a few seconds later. He was in front of a mirror, trying on different jackets.

Patrick was a fuckboy. There was no other way to describe him, maybe manwhore? He liked to sleep around. It got worse when he moved over there, just like I knew it was going to happen. Which was why, before he left three years ago, I made him take a sexual education class since high school failed to give us any useful advice.

"Now you can whore around all you want," I had told him which made him laugh.

Sometimes, I wondered how we were still friends. It had been three years since he left and we lived in different states but somehow, we had made it work. He was all I had.

I talked with him for a while, he told me about his latest hook-up and I listened like the good friend I was. After we hung

5

up, I got in the shower and it was when I was changing that there was a knock on the door.

"Yes?" I called as I threw a blouse over my head.

"Mrs. Collins would like me to tell you that dinner is ready," Katie, one of our maids, called from the other side of the door.

"I'll be right down!" I called back as I put on some jeans. My dad must have gotten here after all. I was excited about seeing him. I missed him whenever he was gone. I finished combing my hair and then quickly made my way out. I ran down the stairs, feeling like a little girl.

"What have I told you about running down the stairs, Hannah?" my mom asked, looking annoyed when I walked into the dining room.

I ignored her and smiled when I saw my dad. My dad was a handsome man. He was tall with broad shoulders and short brown hair with brown eyes and fair skin. I looked like him and I loved it. His smile always took me back to when I was a little girl and he would read to me while I sat on his lap. All of that was gone. He was always flying somewhere nowadays.

"Dad!" I said walking to him.

He stood up as he smiled. "Hey, sweetie," he said as he put his arms around me.

I suddenly had the urge to cry. I missed him so much. "I missed you," I mumbled.

"Me too," he said as he stroked my hair.

"Hannah, your father wants to eat," my mom said sounding annoyed.

I let him go. "Sorry, Dad."

He shook his head. "You okay?" he asked with a frown. His brown eyes studied my face as if trying to read what I had been up to for the past few months.

Oh if only he knew.

I nodded as we took our seats. "Yeah, I just missed you."

He winked at me as he squeezed my hand. I hadn't realized that Nick and his wife, Rachel, were also at the table.

"Hey." Rachel smiled across the table from me.

I smiled at her. "Hey."

I really liked Rachel. She was tall, with long blond hair, hazel eyes, and fair skin. She was not only beautiful but also modest and perfect for my brother. They had been married for about a year and they made the perfect couple. *Literally*, they were always all over the magazines as the perfect couple. Rachel was a fashion designer which was perfect because she fit right in with Nick's business. I admired and wanted to be as good as her someday.

"How was school?" she asked as my mom and dad carried a conversation. I swear she cared more about me than my own mother.

"Good. I'm done for the semester," I said as one of the maids served me pasta. "Thank you," I told her. She smiled. My mom wasn't exactly nice to the housemaids or to anyone who helped keep the house beautiful so I always tried to make up for it.

"What are we talking about?" Nick said looking at Rachel and me. Nick was the spitting image of my mom. They had the same nose, same blond hair, and blue eyes. Nick always kept himself groomed and he was always wearing suits; he fit right in with the bodyguards like camouflage.

Rachel rolled her eyes at him. "So nosy."

He smiled as he leaned in and kissed her on the lips which earned him a glare from my mom who didn't miss anything. *No kissing at the table Nick!*

I smiled at them. They always made me think that true love existed. Up to a few months ago, I thought I had found my true love but all I got was heartbreak instead. Another one added to the list. I was still in the stage where thinking about it still hurt. Thinking about him and everything that happened still made me want to crawl up in a ball and cry.

I never had luck when it came to relationships.

I fell too hard, too fast…and they ended just as fast.

I was starting to believe that maybe love wasn't for me. Maybe I was meant to be alone.

At least I wouldn't hurt that way.

CHAPTER 2

My mom always wanted us to live under the same roof because it *looked good* to be one big, happy family. It worked the first year that we lived here. Then my oldest brother, Colton, got left at the altar and my mom couldn't do anything to stop him from leaving. Now he lives all by himself in the city. It made me wonder if I would have to be left at the altar to leave this house too.

Despite everything, I loved my family but living with my mom was starting to become unbearable. Some days, I *dreaded* coming home. My dad was the only reason I hadn't moved out but with him being gone all the time...well, I was starting to think about moving out. I felt bad for Nick and Rachel. Mostly for Rachel. Nick was my mom's favorite and he had agreed to stay even after he got married. My mom had made him of course, and Nick, to avoid arguments, had agreed to stay. My mom wasn't fond of Rachel. Basically, she wasn't fond of any of my brothers' girlfriends. In her eyes, none of the girls were worthy of them.

"Hannah."

I stopped in my tracks. It was Saturday afternoon, and I was on my way out the door. I wanted to go to the bookstore, my idea of a good Saturday. I turned around, noticing my dad for the first time. He was sitting on the couch with his laptop resting on his lap. I thought he was sleeping considering the fact he had just gotten here last night. I smiled as I walked back to him and kissed his cheek. "Hey, Dad."

"You're going out?" he asked looking at me.

I nodded. "Yeah, I was gonna go find Robin."

He shook his head. "Nathan will be with you today."

9

I gulped at the sound of his name. "But I told you I don't like Nathan," I reminded him.

"Hannah, this isn't about you having to like your bodyguards. It's about your protection, and Nathan is one of the best."

I narrowed my eyes. "But *I don't like him.*"

I sounded like a little girl but I didn't care.

He raised his eyebrow. "Why? Did he do something to you?"

I stared at him for a moment and then finally sighed. "No, he didn't. Whatever, I'm leaving," I said suddenly feeling annoyed.

"Be careful," he called back behind me.

"Yeah," I said before making my way out. Two black cars were parked outside. One of them was empty, and Nathan was standing by the other one.

My hands suddenly felt sweaty and my heart was beating hard against my chest. Maybe I didn't need to go out after all. I could say home, re-read one of the books I had…or read one of the many I had yet to read. I felt guilty going to the bookstore anyway, knowing I had a lot of books in my room I hadn't read.

Suck it up Hannah.

Nathan looked up and met my gaze. To say that I had been avoiding him was an understatement. Ever since he started working here, I always thought he was the most handsome one out of the others. How could he not be? With his perfect height and short brown hair and with those mesmerizing green eyes and muscular arms…He was perfectly good looking.

That wasn't the problem…the problem was that I kissed him. It was a few months ago, right after my breakup, and I hadn't been able to look at him in the eye…until now.

"Ready to go?" he asked me with that stupid amused look he had on his face whenever he talked to me, as if making fun of me. He probably was. He opened the door for me.

10

I nodded. "Yes," I said making my way into the backseat. He shut the door and I followed him with my eyes as he walked around the car and got in the driver's seat.

"Where are we headed?" he asked, glancing at me from the rearview mirror.

I looked down at my lap. "To the bookstore, please."

I reached for my phone and pretended to be texting someone. The ride was quiet, just the sound of Christmas songs playing on the radio. All the cars always had the same radio station, which happened to be the station that switched to playing only Christmas music since November.

This was *not* how I wanted my Saturday to go.

Nathan and I hadn't talked about it ever since it happened. I mean, I was drunk and hurt and he was there...and from what I remembered, he didn't exactly stop me. Maybe I can pretend I didn't remember anything. I *was* drunk after all.

"Hannah?"

I looked up, realizing Nathan had opened the door for me. I hadn't even realized we were here already. "Huh?" I said stupidly.

There was a smile playing on his lips as he looked down at me. "Are you alright?"

"Yeah," I said quickly. "I got it," I said when he offered me his hand but he took my hand anyway and pulled me out of the car. His hand was warm and much bigger than mine. I let it go as soon as I could stand on my feet. But I couldn't seem to look away from his eyes. They were so green and so—amused? He had always been a playful bodyguard. He always seemed to be so happy; I wondered how he did it. What was his secret?

My wallet slipped from my hand and he broke the staring contest to pick it up before it reached the ground. He was fast.

"Thank you," I said as I grabbed it then quickly made my way inside the store.

Just walking in the bookstore made me feel better. It was so cozy and warm with all the shelves of books and the smell of coffee. There was a Starbucks inside so I decided to get a coffee to

11

calm my nerves. I could feel Nathan close behind me as I made my way to it and get in line.

It was in one of these situations that I found bodyguards to be counterproductive. I mean, what a way to draw attention to myself by having a bodyguard shadowing my every step. I could already see the girls sitting at the tables glance at us. Or maybe they were just checking Nathan out.

I took a step back to look at the mugs they had on the stand, when I bumped into Nathan. He placed his hands on my waist to keep me from falling and I immediately took a step away from him, his hands falling at his sides.

"Is it necessary to stand that close?" I demanded quietly.

"Yes, to *protect* you," he said with a smirk.

I rolled my eyes at him as I turned around. I realized it was my turn. I ordered an iced caramel macchiato. After getting my drink, I headed to the romance section, feeling a little embarrassed because Nathan was with me but I tried my best to ignore him. He was probably bored, just standing behind me as I looked at books.

"That guy is gawking at you."

I looked up from reading the back of a book. "What?" I asked turning around.

"*That guy*—" Nathan said raising his eyebrows at someone, "—keeps staring at you."

I followed his gaze. Sure enough, there was a guy sitting on one of the couches they had set up a few feet from where we were standing. He looked down at his book when he noticed us staring.

"*I don't like it,*" Nathan said next to me.

"Yeah, because looks can kill," I told him, rolling my eyes.

He took a step forward. "As your bodyguard, it is my job to tell him to stop."

"Nathan—*wait!*" I hissed but he was already making his way towards the poor guy. I couldn't help but admire how good Nathan looked in that black suit. Was he even real? I watched in amazement as he lowered and told the guy something that made the guy stand up and walk away. I shook my head at him as he made his way back to me. "Unnecessary," I told him but I was fighting back a smile.

"He could have been planning your kidnapping for all we know," he said with a serious face.

"Oh yeah, because everyone around me waste their time planning my kidnapping."

"It's not a waste of time," he said winking at me.

I gulped, feeling my ears get hot. "Shut up," I said because I couldn't think of anything smart to say. I turned around and went back to looking at books but it was impossible to concentrate feeling him close behind me.

Nathan was going to be the death of me. I was an overly attached person that thought big things out of the smallest gestures. That was my problem. I thought way too much and fell too fast.

Nathan wasn't the problem…the problem was *me*.

CHAPTER 3

When Nathan started working for my dad, about two years ago, he became my bodyguard. Like I said, I always thought he was really handsome but that only made me put up even higher walls. Besides, it was pretty much impossible to ignore his good looks. It was easier back then. He was just my bodyguard and I was just some stupid rich girl he had to follow around everywhere.

He was the only one who witnessed my most recent break up. My relationship with Leo never became public. I guess I was happy about it now. But I also understood why he never made the effort to make it public. Leo never really cared about me. He never really loved me, much less like me. That's why I was always the one who had to text him first, always the one to ask him out on dates. I really was blind. And stupid. I humiliated myself like nobody's business and the fact that I knew that now didn't help.

I was so desperate to be loved, to have someone care for me.

I had this whole story made up in my head the moment I saw Leo that I believed it and didn't want to wait for him to do something. *Why did we have to wait for guys to make the first move anyway? Girls could too.* So there I went handing my heart away on a shiny silver platter along with the knife for him to cut right through it. I gave him the power to hurt me, I think that's what hurt most.

Nathan and I never really talked about it but of course he knew—he was always with me. When I asked him not to tell my parents anything about my romance with Leo, he told me not to worry about it. He never broke that promise.

And then I had to go get drunk and kiss him. After that kiss, about four months ago, I asked my dad to change my bodyguard. I told him I didn't like Nathan and he did it without any further questions. I've avoided Nathan ever since. I felt humiliated and embarrassed and hated myself for ever doing it.

"So why do you hate me?" Nathan suddenly asked from behind me as I tried really hard to concentrate on the books.

"I don't hate you," I said calmly, reaching for a book.

"Okay…why don't you like me?"

Oh my god. Couldn't he tell I was trying my best to ignore him? "According to my dad, I don't have to like you in order for you to do your job," I said repeating the exact words my dad had said earlier.

He suddenly leaned in and whispered in my ear, "Is it because the last time we were alone you kissed me?" I could feel his hot breath on my neck sending a shiver run down my spine. I felt tingles in my stomach as the butterflies in there came to life. Good to know they were still alive in there.

"Shut up," I said but it sounded like a plea.

Nathan stood in front of me so I was forced to look at him. He looked completely amused. He really did enjoy making me suffer. "Hannah, come on, we have to talk about it."

"No, we don't," I said, glaring at him. "I was drunk and it was a stupid mistake."

"So you didn't like it?" he asked, a smile playing on his lips.

I opened my mouth but nothing came out. "*Go—wait outside!*" I hissed.

He frowned at me but before he could say anything, his phone began to ring. He reached for it and took a few steps back as he answered. I walked away to another shelf, away from him. He really did like to push my buttons.

By now, I knew I wasn't going to be able to concentrate. Coming here was a bad idea. So I lingered in the gift section of the bookstore. I was there, looking at a snowball, when I looked up and saw Nathan standing a few feet away. The amusement in his eyes was gone. For once, he looked completely serious as he stared at me with his green eyes.

"Nathan?" I asked walking to him when he didn't move. "What's wrong?"

"It was your father," he said slowly.

By the look on his face, I knew it wasn't a casual call. It was bad news, I felt it. "What's wrong?" I repeated. "Nathan please say something."

"Your brother—"

"Colton?" I didn't know why I thought of him first. I guess it was because I hadn't seen him in a really long time.

Nathan had a look of dread on his face. "Nick was shot. He's in the hospital, having surgery."

"What?" I asked feeling my eyes get wide in horror. "What happened? Is he—" My throat tightened and I suddenly couldn't talk anymore. It felt like I couldn't breathe.

Nathan placed his hands on my shoulders. "I don't know but if you let me—I'll take you to the hospital."

I nodded, not being able to say anything. He led me to the car and for once, I was glad that he didn't let my hand go, knowing that I would have fallen if he did. He opened the passenger door for me.

"Just go, hurry!" I said when he reached for my seatbelt. So he would move, I reached over and pulled the seatbelt over my chest. Nathan shut the door and hurried to the driver's seat. He drove like a maniac, speeding past all the other cars and making illegal turns but I was glad. I needed to get to the hospital. Nick couldn't be dead. I just had dinner with him last night.

I kept gulping, trying to make the knot in my throat disappear. But it wouldn't go. It stayed there, threatening to make me cry any second. It was one of the things I hated about myself.

I cried if I was *too anything*. I cried if I was *too happy, too sad, too mad, too confused, too scared.*

When we got to the hospital, there was already a group of men with big cameras outside the doors, taking pictures, talking on

16

the phone, waiting. It made me sick to my stomach. I couldn't deal with them right now. My brother was shot and all they cared about was getting good money for a photo.

The car stopped and they all began to hover over it, snapping pictures with their expensive cameras, making it too bright for me to see anything.

"Get the hell out of the way!" I heard Nathan yell at them when he got out. He opened the door, pushing a few of them to the side to do it. He took off his jacket and looked at me. "Trust me okay?"

I nodded, closing my eyes.

I felt him put the jacket over my head as I got out of the car then he placed his hand on the back of my head and pressed me to his chest. His other hand went around me, making sure I wasn't touched as we walked. I didn't know where I was going so I let him lead me. Amazingly, no one even touched me.

Once we got inside, Nathan let me go. "Are you okay?"

I nodded. "Thanks."

He grabbed my hand. "Come on."

We got on the elevator and Nathan led me to the waiting room where my family was. My parents were sitting next to each other and Rachel was on the floor, with her knees brought up to her chest. For the first time my mom was actually quiet, looking down at the floor.

My dad stood up when he saw me and enveloped me in a hug, it was then when I broke down crying. The first sob was loud but I didn't care about embarrassing myself. I cried into my dad's chest as he ran his hand down my hair over and over.

"He's okay. He's in surgery," he said after a moment.

"What happened?" I choked out cleaning the tears on my cheeks. My dad led me to the chairs and we sat down.

"Someone shot him while he was in his office," my dad said quietly. "We still don't know who it was. It was after hours so he was alone in the office. Thankfully, Rachel wasn't with him or she could have gotten hurt too." He shook his head at the thought.

17

"The police are investigating. They'll be checking the cameras but if it was an insider that knew about them, then there isn't much hope…"

"Oh my God," I whispered. "Why would someone do that to Nick?" A million things were running through my head. Nick didn't have any enemies—at least from what I knew. I liked to think he was a kind boss.

My dad shrugged, looking helpless. He looked 10 years older than how he looked this morning. So much for a day of relaxation.

"What is it, Dad," I asked. I could tell there was something bothering him.

"Nothing, honey. We all just chose careers that gives our lives a lot of exposure. It's not always a good thing. Maybe this was a tragedy waiting to happen."

I didn't know what to say to him because I agreed with him. I wished he would have never become an actor. Why couldn't he be a lawyer or an engineer? Our lives would be a little easier. But there was no point in reminiscing about what could have been. Besides, it wasn't all his fault. Nick had chosen a dangerous career as well. Maybe he did have enemies? Someone wanted his position? I didn't know enough about Nick's colleagues to guess anything. Maybe it was an angry ex-employee? Maybe he wasn't a kind boss after all.

I noticed there were bodyguards all around the floor, along with a few cops. My dad stood up and went to talk with them and my eyes landed on Rachel who was crying. I stood up and sat down next to her.

I didn't tell her anything. I was just as scared as she was.

"Where's Colton?" I asked my mom.

She didn't look at me but answered. "He won't pick up the phone."

I took out my phone and dialed Colton, praying he would answer.

18

"Hannah?"

"Colton! Where the hell are you?" I hissed.

He sounded out of breath and I wondered what he was doing. Hopefully working out. I *hoped* working out. Lately, he had been sleeping around a lot. He hadn't always been like that. Colton started sleeping around after he got left at the altar. I guess it was his way to deal with it. Not the best way, if you ask me.

"I just heard," he said sounding distracted. "How is he?"

The tears began to roll down my cheeks again and Rachel squeezed my hand. "I don't know," I whispered. "I'm so scared."

Colton sighed. "I'm sure he's going to be okay, Hannah. I'm on my way, okay?"

I nodded then remembered he couldn't see me and whispered, "Okay."

I didn't know how much time passed after that. I saw Nathan spoke to my dad before he left. A minute later, I saw dad speaking with the cops. Everything was a blur. Colton arrived shortly.

Colton and Nick looked a lot alike, they could easily be twins except that Colton dyed his hair black after the whole wedding thing but they had the same eyes, they were both tall, and they were both always wearing suits. Of course, Colton looked a little older than him but that was it.

I didn't know how much time had passed before the doctor finally came out to speak with us. Rachel and I got to our feet. The doctor told my dad something and I watched as my dad's shoulders relaxed.

Relief swept through my body, making me feel a thousand pounds lighter.

Nick was going to be okay. He was still weak but just needed to rest. I hugged Rachel as she actually laughed while she cried.

And then my dad turned to me. "Hannah, I think it's safer for you to get out of New York for some time."

And my life changed just like that.

19

CHAPTER 4

I looked out the window as the car sped down the street. I could catch sight of the people in the other cars driving past us. They were probably doing normal things like going home from work or going to the movies while I was trying to escape danger.

I glanced at Nathan as he drove before looking down at my lap before he caught me looking at him. I wondered how much he knew. Probably more than my dad had told me. I thought back to our conversation earlier in the hospital after he told me he thought it was best for me to leave the city.

"But why?" I asked him with a confused frown on my forehead.

"It's just not safe here, Hannah."

"It's not safe for anyone, dad. What about mom? Rachel? Colton? Are they going away too?"

"No."

I waited for him to give me an explanation about why I was the only one that had to leave but he didn't. I held his gaze. Brown eyes to brown eyes. It seemed like he had aged years since this morning.

"I don't get it." I finally told him. "Why just me?"

I was a little hurt that he wanted me to go away because I wanted to say here with him and Nick and the rest of my family. What safer place than with them? This tragedy still had me shaken. I knew Nick was going to be okay but that didn't mean that we could just ignore what had happened to him. Someone was out there, trying to hurt my family. Maybe going away *was* a good idea but all of us together.

20

My dad sighed, looking tired, then he grabbed my arm and pulled me to the side away from mom and Rachel and Colton. I noticed Robin, the bodyguard, take a few steps with us but he still kept his distance, giving us privacy.

"I received a phone call," my dad said in a low voice.

"Okay…" I said slowly but feeling a bit impatient.

"The voice on the other end…" he hesitated.

"Dad, please just tell me."

"They said that you were next." My dad looked bothered and angry as he said that. The words didn't seem to come out the way he wanted them to. I was sure he didn't know how to tell me this.

"That I was next?" I repeated and then realization hit me. "Oh."

I was next on their hit list. Why? What did I do? What did Nick do? What the hell was going on? Why would someone want to hurt my family? With what purpose?

"The man didn't give me a chance to say anything. I was still processing what he had told me when I realized that the call had disconnected." The words slipped out of my dad's mouth quickly. "The police know and they're working on tracking the call though there's not much hope because they probably used a disposable phone. It also doesn't help that the only recorded evidence of the call is the voice that keeps repeating in my head."

I shook my head. "I don't want to go anywhere. I want to stay here."

"Hannah, please try to understand. There is someone out there who almost killed your brother and it now trying to target you. I don't know who it is or how serious they are with this threat but I am not jeopardizing your safety." He looked around us then lowered his voice. "We don't know how close this individual is to us. It could be *anyone*."

"But me leaving the city is not the solution—"

"It is for now." He interrupted.

"Where would I even go?"

21

"Anywhere. Just get out of the city and on land. No plane. The less people that know the better. You will leave with Nathan."

I shook my head again. "No, dad, please don't make me leave."

"Hannah, I am not compromising your safety. This will be temporary. Please try to understand me."

He was desperate. I could see it in his eyes. He just wanted me to be safe and I understood. The problem was that I didn't know what terrified me more: being alone without or my family or leaving them here with the chance of someone else becoming the target. The thought of something happening to my dad scared me and it made me want to cry. My dad put his arms around me tightly.

"Stay with your bodyguard at all times. Do not leave his side and please do as he says. I trust Nathan will keep you safe," he said onto my ear.

Now in the car, all I could think about was whether that would be the last time I would be able to hug my dad. Well that and the fact that I would be alone with Nathan for God knows how many days. It was incredulous. I had a death threat and the thought of being alone with my bodyguard still made me more nervous...it even excited me a bit. There must be something wrong with me.

"Hannah?"

I looked up at the sound of my name and met Nathan's green eyes on the rearview mirror. He had stopped at a red light. "Huh?"

"Have you decided where we are going?"

I shrugged as I looked out the window again. "The only place I can think of where I would want to be is with my best friend."

"I'm going to need a bit more information here," Nathan said as he drove.

I sighed. "Patrick lives in Miami. Want to drive there?"

"We can."

I looked at him. "That's a lot of driving." At the same time, I Googled how many hours it was to drive from New York to Miami.

19h and 1m

It was like Google was mocking me with that extra minute. Adding a few gas and food stops, it would take about a day to get there. A day alone with my bodyguard. The same bodyguard that I drunk kissed and have been ignoring for weeks.

"We can go anywhere, Hannah, as long as we're together."

I looked away, feeling heat creep on the back of my neck. What was wrong with me? He obviously said that in a very non-romantic way. He was my bodyguard; he was *supposed* to be with me.

Thankfully, he didn't seem to notice my blush. I was glad he was driving, it meant he had to focus on doing that. I leaned my head on the window and closed my eyes. I was trying to get some sleep but couldn't. I could feel Nathan glancing at me a few times but I ignored him. When I checked the time, only two hours had passed since we left the hospital.

"Do you mind if we get something to eat?" I asked suddenly feeling hungry. Maybe it was the nerves.

Nathan nodded, keeping his eyes on the road. "I'll get out the next exit."

I watched as he kept moving to the left lanes until he reached the last one and got out. There was a fast food restaurant and I told Nathan we could just eat there. When he parked, I didn't wait for him to open the door and just got out.

It was a chilly night. I crossed my arms in my chest. I felt Nathan place a sweater on my shoulders. When I realized it was mine, I frowned. This sweater was in my closet this morning.

"Your father sent me to pack you some clothes," Nathan explained.

I blushed. He saw my underwear. My *granny panties*.

Nathan chuckled. "Just another secret I'll keep," he teased as if he was reading my mind.

I looked down at my feet as we walked inside the restaurant. "Who do you think shot Nick?" I asked him, eager to change the subject.

He shrugged. "There are infinite possibilities. There is not much that we know at the moment." He looked at me. "You can't be angry at your dad for trying to protect you."

I bit my lower lip. "Do you think the threat my dad received is real?"

I didn't know why I wanted to hear what his thoughts were on this. Maybe because I knew Nathan was an optimist. He made everything seem less serious. I never thought I would find myself seeking relief in that.

He stared at me for a moment and I wondered what was going through his head. "I think it's better to be safe than sorry."

I nodded slowly, looking away. "Right."

We waited in line in silence. It seemed to take forever before we finally ordered and then a little more for us to get our food. After we finally got our food, we sat down on one of the booths. The people that were there were just leaving and I silently thanked them. I was tired of standing up.

I didn't waste time and bit off the cheeseburger as soon as I sat down. I knew I was eating fast but I didn't care, I was too hungry. Before I knew it, the cheeseburger was gone and only the fries were left.

"So," Nathan said as he reached for a fry. "How are you?"

I frowned at his question. "Okay?" He had asked me that a hundred times from the moment we left the hospital.

"Really?"

"Why do you say it like that?" I asked, dipping some fries in the ketchup and then putting them in my mouth.

"Because I know you," he said with a shrug as if we were old friends.

"No, you don't," I said, suddenly feeling annoyed.

"I do," he said, sounding confident.

24

"You are my bodyguard, Nathan, we've rarely talked. This—" I waved my index finger between him and me, "—is the most we've ever talked."

"But I *notice* everything about you." He looked at me with his intense green eyes.

I looked down then back up at him. "Enlighten me," I said, crossing my arms in my chest. I told myself that I was just looking for a distraction but deep down, I knew I wanted to hear what he had noticed about me.

He leaned in over the table. "You only have one friend, Patrick. You talk to people at school but you don't really hang out with them. You read in your free time. You love drawing, you're really good by the way. You used to laugh at everything, don't try to deny it. You used to always complain about it. But that changed after..." he trailed off but he held my gaze.

I didn't say anything for a moment as my gaze dropped to the table. I didn't know what to say or think. I knew he probably didn't mean it that way but that was the most romantic thing anyone had ever said to me. And of course, only *I* would find that romantic.

Leo never noticed anything about me. I guess it made sense. Before Leo, Nathan was always with me. He had to, it was his job. It just never occurred to me that he noticed things.

"After Leo," I finished for him. "It's okay."

"I know you don't like talking about it," he said slowly

"Thank you for reminding me that I'm a loner by the way," I joked, trying to lighten the mood. Whether I liked it or not, I was stuck with Nathan for the next couple of days and the last thing I wanted was to make things awkward between us. "And you're also a creep."

He chuckled. "It's not like I had a choice."

"Geez. Sorry for being such a burden," I said, making him roll his eyes at me. My phone rang then. It was Colton. I had asked him to keep me posted on Nick. Everything was fine. He still hadn't opened his eyes but the doctor said he was stable and would be okay.

"Nick is going to be fine," I said, mostly to myself, then frowned as I put my phone down. "You know, I hadn't seen Colton since the wedding. Isn't it sad that something like this had to happen for my family to come together?"

"At least you know they'll be there if something happens," Nathan said easily.

I fought back a smile. "Why do you always do that?"

"Do what?"

"Look at the bright side of things. It's annoying." I teased him.

He chuckled. "Sorry for being an optimist?"

"I think it's better to look at things the way they are: black and white. You know, be realistic," I said looking down at the table, trying to hide the pain behind my words.

"But the world isn't black and white," He said softly. "There are colors everywhere...*You* are a color, Hannah." He cleared his throat. "Everyone is."

So optimism was Nathan's secret to always been in a happy mood. Well, there you go. The key to happiness. Now I had to figure out how to become an optimist.

I looked up at him and moved my head to the side. "Why are you always so nice to me?"

He half smiled. "I know you've been hurting and I've made it my mission to make you smile again." He winked at me.

I half smiled but didn't say anything and I was glad he didn't either. Nathan talked too much sometimes and he said things that made my heart flutter and that was dangerous. We finished eating in silence and then headed back to the car. Except for the car's headlights, the road was dark ahead of us. It almost looked like the scene of a scary movie. Okay, it *did* look like the scene of a scary movie but I was trying not to think about that.

I didn't know how much time passed or how it happened but Nathan was driving straight ahead and I was just starting to find my sleep again, my heavy eyelids were closing slowly when something hard hit the car.

CHAPTER 5

My hands gripped the seat as the car began to glide around in circles. My eyes were open; it made me feel dizzy and sick to my stomach so I shut my eyes tightly and braced myself for the worst. I felt the car hit something, making it bolt forward, if it weren't for my seatbelt, I'm positive I would have ended up crashing through the windshield.

The car suddenly came to a complete stop and then there was an utter silence.

I couldn't hear anything and I was too scared to open my eyes. Until I felt someone—Nathan grab me by the shoulders and I felt him squeeze me. I opened my eyes and stared into his green eyes. He was shouting but I couldn't hear anything. *Why was he so angry? Why couldn't I hear anything?* I must be in shock. And then, slowly, I began to hear again.

"Hannah! Are you alright? God, please say something!" Nathan was shouting at me.

"*What*—happened?" I blurted out. The only thing illuminating us was the light in the car. Everything else was dark. I could smell gasoline and burnt tire.

"Oh, thank God," Nathan sighed in relief. "A car hit us. Are you alright?" he asked, his green eyes scanning my body. "Can you stand? We can't stay here."

I felt seriously sick. Scared that I would throw up on him, I just nodded then began to stand up. My knees felt weak. I had never been in a car accident before and I knew I was lucky to not have a single scratch…so far.

Nathan put an arm around my waist, as if he were unsure that I was able to walk. I was unsure myself. When I took the first step, I felt the food go up my throat and I halted. I threw up on the poor grass.

Oh God. This is so embarrassing.

"Are you alright?" Nathan asked behind me after I stopped.

"I think so..." I said straightening up. Surprisingly enough, I did feel much better. Nathan handed me a water bottle and I washed my mouth a few times, spitting the water out. The aftertaste was still there, but it was a little less. That was so gross. I hated throwing up. It was the worst thing ever.

I looked around and realized that the only reason the car stopped was because it hit a tree. The tree was huge and didn't seem to be damaged at all, except for a few scratches from where the car struck it. Unfortunately, I couldn't say the same thing about the car. It looked bad. The hood was out of place and smoke was coming out of it, it made me wonder how Nathan had gotten out without a scratch.

"Where's the other car?" I wondered, looking around. We were in a two-way street and there were no cars coming in either way. We were in the middle of nowhere with no one in sight.

"It was a stupid truck," Nathan said, sounding angry as he opened the trunk of the car. "And they drove away."

"Nathan..." I said slowly. He looked up at me, alarmed. "We are in the middle of nowhere...where are we going to go?"

I was scared. It was freezing and it was dark, and we didn't have a car. We were in the middle of nowhere and there was nobody that could help us. I could feel my body begin to tremble though it was more because of my nerves than the cold.

Nathan walked to me and began to run his hands up and down my shoulders. His touch was comforting. "Breathe, Hannah. You have nothing to worry about. I won't let anything happen to you," he promised.

"That doesn't make me feel better," I told him bluntly.

29

He chuckled softly. "Well, I mean it. Whatever happens, we'll get through it."

I didn't know what else to say, I still didn't feel safe but at least I wasn't alone. Maybe Nathan's confidence would save us tonight. I just nodded and he went back to the trunk of the car. I watched as he took out a suitcase and a duffel bag, which he threw over his shoulder.

"What are you doing?" I asked even though I already knew the answer.

"We can't stay here. I have no service so we have to walk—see if we can find something or someone." He looked at me. "We can't stay here," he said again as if trying to convince himself that it was a good idea to leave.

I didn't really have a Plan B. I knew he was right. So I followed him when he began walking. I took out my phone but I didn't have any service either. When I needed the phone more than ever, it bailed. We walked in silence for a moment. Just the sound of the suitcase wheels rolling behind us and the occasional cold breeze that made me shake all over.

What the hell was happening? First Nick gets shot and now we get in an accident. Can we stop it with the inconveniences please? *I want my nothing-ever-happens boring life back. I won't complain anymore, I promise.*

"We are going to have to spend the night here," Nathan said after a moment.

We had walked a few miles, I could no longer see the car behind us but I could see smoke and knew it was probably burning. I prayed that someone passed by it and called the police. I didn't contradict Nathan, mostly because I was exhausted and just wanted to sit down for a moment. For the first time, I was glad that it was him who had come with me. At least I knew him better than the other bodyguards. The person I've avoided for months is the only one I have right now. *How ironic?*

He led us into the woods, took out a tiny flashlight from the key chain and moved it around. We didn't walk too much when

30

he stopped at a log; I could still see the street from where we were. I watched as Nathan opened up the duffel bag and took out his, probably expensive, suits and began to place them on the ground.

"Nathan, that's not necessary," I said sheepishly when I realized what he was doing.

"Yes, it is," he said, glancing at me and offering me a smile.

Despite everything, he was still nice to me. I didn't deserve it, but I let him sit me down on the hard ground and help me lean back on the log. He took out the clothes that were on the suitcase and threw them all over me. He started shuffling in the dark and I sat there, squinting my eyes, trying to see what he was doing until he lighted up a small fire in front of us with some sticks. *How was he able to do that?*

I was shaking uncontrollably. I liked the cold weather, yes, but not so much when I had to spend the night in the middle of nowhere and the only heat was coming from a small fire. Nathan sat next to me. He was only wearing his black jacket.

"H-How are y-you not freezing?" I asked through chattering teeth.

He grinned at me and then put his arm around my shoulders. "May I?" he asked politely.

I nodded desperately, already feeling the heat radiating from his body. He was hot. *Literally*, hot. Nick and Colton were like him, always warm. Not me. I was a corpse in the winter. My feet were always cold no matter what. His arm went around my shoulders and he pulled me closer to him. I put my arm around his hard torso and buried my face in his chest. He was so warm.

"Better?" he whispered.

I didn't want to move away from him so I just nodded. We sat in silence for a moment. I began to feel my face and arms again. When I did look up, I noticed he was cleaning blood from his forehead with his free hand.

"You're hurt," I said, noticing the cut on his forehead. I hadn't even realized that he was bleeding. All this time, all he cared about was me.

31

"I'm okay," he assured me.

"You're so nice to me. Why are you so nice to me?" I asked him for the second time that night.

He chuckled. Listening to his laugh was actually comforting. "Why would I not?"

I looked down. "Because I haven't been exactly nice to you."

"You haven't," he agreed with me.

"I haven't really been myself lately," I said out of nowhere.

"You haven't," he agreed again.

I looked up at him. The small light from the fire illuminated his face. He looked...*well*...he looked beautiful. His skin looked soft and bright in the darkness. "Was it really that obvious?"

"It was to me," he said looking straight ahead.

"I'm not a very decent person, am I?"

"You are actually one of the best people I know," I felt him shrug. "Pain changes us. Pain changed you and it's okay. Nothing out of this world."

I didn't know what to say, so I just kept quiet.

"It was all okay, until the part where you decided to take me out of your life," he said after a moment.

"Yeah, I don't want to talk about that," I said, feeling bad for treating him the way I have for the past few months.

"What should we talk about then? We are spending the night in the woods. If this isn't the perfect time to talk, then I don't know when is."

"I don't want to talk about *him*..." I whispered. Or my love life in general. It was just sad. *Heartbreak after heartbreak...*

"Why not?"

"Because it hurts, Nathan. You have no idea how much it hurts."

He stared into my eyes. His gaze was so intense that it was impossible for me to look away. His eyes softened after a moment...there was a little sadness in them as he whispered,

32

"Oh, I think I do."

CHAPTER 6

The moon was nowhere in sight tonight, but the sky was full of stars. They seemed so close, I wanted to reach with my hand and see if I could catch one. There wasn't anyone or anything in sight. It was just Nathan and I alone in the middle of the woods, trees all around us. I wondered what time it was, but I was too comfortable in Nathan's arms to move. He smelled so good. He *felt* so good.

"It would be okay, you know," Nathan said next to me. "If you wanted to talk."

"I haven't talked about him since it happened," I whispered then I gulped. "Mostly because I'm embarrassed by all the things I did for him. He never cared about me," I looked up at him. "Did you know? Could you see it?"

"It was none of my business," he said after a moment.

I shook my head in disbelief. "I fell too hard and too fast. Like I always do...I was the one that had to text him. Otherwise, we wouldn't talk. *I* was the one who would ask *him* out on dates." My laugh was dry. "You must think I'm an idiot."

He shrugged. "You were in love. People do crazy things when they're in love. There is nothing wrong with that."

I smiled at him. "There is everything wrong with getting drunk and kissing your bodyguard."

A smile was playing on his lips. "No, actually, there is nothing wrong with that. What is wrong, though, is making your dad remove your bodyguard from your service and making him feel like he did something wrong."

I rolled my eyes at him. "Why would you think that? *I* was the one that kissed *you*."

"Yes, and then you stopped talking to me."

"We didn't even talk!" I teased.

"And here I was thinking we had a friendship going on."

I actually laughed. "I was just embarrassed, Nathan. You were the only one that witnessed my humiliation, and then I get drunk and kiss you and humiliate myself some more."

"I wasn't going to judge you," he said softly. "I knew you were drunk and I knew you were hurt. You didn't do anything wrong. You did what every hurt person would do."

I frowned. "Really? I didn't know everyone went on and kissed their bodyguards when they get their hearts broken."

"Oh, it's totally a thing."

We laughed quietly. It was then that I realized that I was in the middle of nowhere, spending the night in the woods and I was actually having a good time. Of course, Nathan had something to do with it. He made me feel good about myself. He hadn't judged me.

I felt completely safe.

And warm.

And I wasn't panicking.

The fact that Nathan had *everything* to do with it, scared me. I couldn't remember the last time someone made me feel like this. *Safe. Good. Happy.*

"Are you okay?" Nathan whispered, bringing me back to reality.

"Yeah," I whispered back, burying my face in his shoulder so he wouldn't see my face. "What time is it?"

I felt him bring his right arm closer, pushing me against him so he could check his watch. "Uh, four something," He placed his hand on my shoulder, moving it up and down.

"Nathan?" I whispered.

"Yes?"

"You're not as bad as I thought."

35

His chest vibrated as he laughed.

~

I didn't fall asleep. I was way too uncomfortable. Not because of Nathan, he was the only good part, the problem was my butt. I couldn't feel it. Or my legs. But I didn't want to move. I didn't want him to let me go. It wasn't long before we watched the sunrise. I had never been so happy to see the sun before.

"My butt is numb," I said after there was enough light to see what was in front of me. We had really made it through the night in one piece.

Nathan laughed. "Mine is too."

It was time. Slowly, we untangled from each other and pulled apart. I suddenly felt cold, but I had to stand up, see if my legs still worked. It felt good to stretch. I helped Nathan pick up the clothes and put them back in the suitcase and duffel bag. Then we hit the road again.

"What now?"

"We see if we can get a car to stop for us."

"So we're hitchhiking."

"Yes."

I glanced at him. "That's dangerous."

He rolled his green eyes at me. "We spend the night in the middle of nowhere and you think hitchhiking is dangerous?"

I laughed. "You're right, I guess. Besides, I have my own personal bodyguard to protect me, right?"

He looked at me and smiled. "Right. I won't let anything happen to you, Hannah. Not for as long as I breathe."

We stared at each other for a moment. I hadn't even realized we had stopped walking until I started walking again. "We'll just have to make sure you don't die then," I said as I looked away, making him laugh.

We walked in silence for a moment. "Where are we?" I wondered.

"We're probably still in New York," Nathan said with a frown.

36

"At this rate, we'll reach Miami in a week."

"No kidding," Nathan said, flashing me a smile.

"Why do you like me?" I blurted out without thinking. I think it was the way he smiled at me…as if he wouldn't mind spending a whole week with me.

"What?" he asked, looking embarrassed.

I laughed. "Why do you like being my bodyguard?"

"Oh." He cleared his throat as he looked straight ahead. "You're the better Collins."

"What does that mean?" I asked with a frown.

"Do I have permission to talk *not-so-nice* about your family?"

I shrugged. "I do it all the time."

He chuckled. "Well, your mother is hard to be around with. She kind of treats us like dogs. The rest of your family—well, I just don't find them interesting." I laughed and he turned to look at me and smiled. "You're the only normal one. And you're modest and humble. That makes you likable."

"Likable isn't a word." I laughed.

Or was it? I had no idea. It sounded like slang.

He chuckled then looked at me again. "Pretty sure it is, Collins."

I smiled as I looked straight ahead. "I've always thought that I was the boring Collins, turns out I was right."

Nathan hesitated. "I didn't mean it like that."

"I know," I said with a sad smile. "It's just—my brothers all lived up to our name. They all have successful careers, and then there's me—just basic Hannah."

With the unsuccessful career and unsuccessful love life.

"Only you see yourself like that," Nathan said softly. He turned to look at me. "You're my favorite Collins if that makes you feel any better."

I smiled at the road in front of me.

It did.

CHAPTER 7

"I am hungry."

I didn't know how long we had been walking for. It felt like hours had passed. The sun was barely reaching its position high up in the sky. Two cars had passed, but none of them stopped for us. *I* wouldn't stop for us. People probably thought we were some dangerous runaways or something. I found myself imagining Nathan and me as runaways…we wanted to be together, but my family wouldn't allow it…so we ran away together. He was my bodyguard—it was a forbidden love. How romantic.

God. I needed to stop making up stories in my head.

I looked at Nathan and glared at him. "You don't look tired at all."

He grinned. "We are trained for this kind of stuff. Besides I *do* exercise, you know," he teased.

I shrugged. "I'm not even going to fight you on that. I am a fat ass that doesn't like exercise, that's a fact."

He looked behind me. "*It is* a nice fat ass."

I felt my ears grow hot as I slapped his arm, playfully making him laugh.

"Hey! I have a signal!" Nathan said after a moment when he checked his phone. He stopped as if afraid the signal might go away if he moved.

"Oh my god!" I said in relief. "Call a pizza!"

He turned to look at me with an amused look on his face. "What?"

I blushed. "I'm sorry—I'm just really hungry. Just call someone, please," I said waving my hands at him so he would hurry up.

He chuckled and then frowned. "I have to call your father."

Without another word, he dialed and put the phone on his ear with a dreaded look on his face. The conversation began with *"we got hit by a car but we are okay"* followed by a very serious Nathan saying, "I understand sir," over and over. Knowing my dad, he was probably yelling at him when it wasn't even Nathan's fault. I couldn't take it anymore and snatched the phone from Nathan.

"Dad, we are fine!"

"Hannah?" My dad sounded confused.

"I am fine. Nothing happened to me. This isn't Nathan's fault. Now, can you just send someone to help us because I'm freaking starving!"

Nathan began to laugh quietly next to me, but I ignored him. I was tired and hungry and thirsty. This was serious.

"Uh, yes, sweetie. I'm going to send some help and then you and Nathan can continue on your way. Are you sure you feel safe with him?"

I turned to look at Nathan who had been staring at me and smiled. "Yes, I'm sure. Now hurry before I starve to death," I said then hung up. I sent him our location over text.

"You're scary when you're hungry," Nathan told me as I handed him his phone.

I rolled my eyes at him. "Please tell me they'll be here soon."

"Are you going to hurt me if I say it'll be a few hours?"

"I might eat you," I joked then laughed at the expression on his face. *Wow. I was so bad at flirting.*

"There's a car coming," he said after a moment as he turned around. I didn't know how he could tell. I didn't see anything.

"I got an idea," Nathan said taking off his jacket. I watched as he rolled it into a ball and then he pulled up my shirt and pushed it in there before I even had time to react. It wasn't until he pulled my shirt down that I realized what he had done. I looked down at my now pregnant-looking belly just in time for the car to miraculously stop in front of us.

The driver, a nice-looking old lady, rolled down the window and looked at me. "You guys need help?" she asked me, eyeing my belly. Her husband, I guessed, was in the passenger seat. They looked like nice people, I felt bad about lying.

At the same time, it took all my might for me to not crack up laughing.

Nathan placed his hand on my back. "Uh, yeah, we had some car trouble. We're just trying to get somewhere. The nearest gas station or something?"

"Yes, yes, of course!" the old man said. "Hop on!"

Nathan winked at me then opened the back door for me. I got in then he put the suitcases in the trunk and climbed in.

"Thank you so much," I said, feeling guilty.

"No worries, sweetie," the old lady said as she drove. "Are you hurt? Is the baby okay?"

I pulled my sweater closer to me. "No, I'm—we're okay. Thank you."

"Are you two married?" the lady asked, glancing at us through the rearview mirror.

"Yes," Nathan answered calmly, putting his arm around me. "We were actually heading to our second honeymoon."

I turned to glare at him, but he just smiled. He seemed so confident lying, it scared me a bit.

"Well, you make a lovely couple! And you are going to have a baby! A baby is always a blessing."

"It is indeed," Nathan said winking at me. I shook my head with a smile and looked out the window to hide my guilty face.

He carried on a conversation with her, who seemed to be a more talkative person, unlike her husband who fell asleep during the ride. It was a while before we finally reached a rest stop. I didn't know if it seemed long because of her slow driving or because we really were far, but we finally reach a rest stop, and we got out. She waved at us as she drove away. I had an urge to tell her that she shouldn't pick up random strangers in the streets because it was dangerous but I bit my tongue.

I turned to look at Nathan and shook my head.

"What?" he asked when I kept giving him the look.

"You got me pregnant!" I hissed, taking out the sweater.

"It was either that, or you would have eaten me alive!" he said, looking amused.

"True," I admitted then laughed. "Let's go eat!"

I didn't wait for him and began to make my way to the first restaurant I saw. It was a breakfast inn, but I didn't care. I just needed food. We sat at a booth and ordered. I was a happy camper because they didn't take forever to bring the food.

"You don't mind eating in front of me," Nathan said as we ate.

"Why would I be?" I asked before putting another forkful of pancakes in my mouth.

"That's a first, Collins. I hate going on dates because all the girls just seem so uncomfortable eating in front of me. Once, one of them ordered spaghetti and didn't even touch it because she was too embarrassed to get dirty. Like I'm going to judge someone for eating." He shook his head, looking confused.

I stared at him for a moment. Nathan was a really handsome guy. Chris Hemsworth handsome. Henry Cavill handsome. *Hollywood* handsome. It didn't take a genius to understand why girls would be embarrassed to eat in front of him.

"Well, you are not ugly, Nathan."

He smirked. "Are you calling me sexy?"

Oh, if only he could read my mind...

I rolled my eyes at him. "Don't flatter yourself. This isn't a date. Besides, you're not handsome enough to keep *me* from eating in front of *you*," I teased him, laughing as his face fell in disbelief.

"So do you have a girlfriend?" I asked casually though I had been dying to ask.

"When exactly would I have time to have a girlfriend?" he asked, looking down at his food.

"On your day off?"

"I don't have a day off."

I frowned. "Why are you always working? Don't you have a family or something?"

He narrowed his eyes at me. "You have a family, but any chance you get, you wanna escape from them."

"Okay, you have a point," I said slowly. "Do you have a family, though?"

"I do…" He avoided my gaze.

"But?" I pushed when he didn't say anything.

"I'm not close to them," he said with a shrug. "My mom remarried when I was ten years old. She had other children with him, but I never got along with them. My father died in the war."

I looked at him, but he was looking down. So I reached over and placed my hand on top of his to make him look at me. "Your dad was amazing for what he did."

His green eyes bore into mine as he gave me a crooked grin. "*You're* kind of amazing."

I felt a warm feeling in my stomach and I froze, trying to enjoy the feeling. And then I shook it off. I looked down instead and kept eating.

I hated it when he looked at me like that. It felt like he could see right through me. He was not supposed to make me feel this way. He wasn't supposed to say things like that. He wasn't supposed to care. He was my bodyguard. My father's employee. He was getting paid for this. I needed to remember that.

"So how long do you think we have to wait?" I asked instead, trying to change the subject.

"I'd say about two, three hours. Maybe more."

I sighed, taking a sip of the fresh water. "I. Am. So. Full," I said slowly.

"That's what happens when you eat fast," he teased.

I smiled at him. "You know, I used to not like you."

It wasn't entirely true. I didn't like how I felt being around him because he had always made me nervous though that wasn't entirely his fault. I'm sure he was guilty of making many women nervous.

"Really?" he raised his eyebrows. "What do you think of me now?"

"I don't know yet."

He leaned across the table until he was right in front of me. His green eyes roamed all over my face and they stop on my lips for a moment. He smiled. "Let me know when you figure it out, Collins, because I'm not going anywhere."

CHAPTER 8

I opened my eyes to an unfamiliar room.

Where was I?

I rolled over the bed as I started to remember where I was. After breakfast, Nathan insisted on booking a room in the hotel across the diner so I could get some sleep. I didn't protest. I was tired and now, I was waking up to a lonely room.

The room was very simple, nothing fancy. There was a TV across the bed, standing on top of a drawer, a small brown couch and a heater over by the wall. I noticed that my phone was charging on the nightstand. I didn't remember plugging it. Nathan must have done it.

I stood up and got in the shower. After I got out, I spent about ten minutes brushing my teeth over and over. Then I changed into jeans with a red, long-sleeved blouse and my sneakers. I was combing my hair when my phone began to ring.

"Hello?" I asked as I tried to put on my sweater.

"Hannah! Where the hell are you? Why haven't you been answering your phone?" Patrick yelled in my ear.

"I'm sorry my phone died," I said, putting on my scarf. "We were in a car crash and—"

"Wait—what? Are you okay?"

"Yes, nothing serious but we did lose the car. We're going to be there a little later than anticipated," I concluded.

"Who's we?" he asked.

Oh, no. Here it goes. "Oh, me and my bodyguard," I said casually.

"*Oh?*" I could hear the smile in his voice. "Your bodyguard?" I could almost see the stupid smirk on his face.

I smiled, unable to keep my cool. "Patrick, shut up! It's not like that."

"How is it then?"

I rolled my eyes. "We are not talking about this."

"Fine. You can tell me when you get here. I can't wait to see you."

I smiled. "I know. Me either."

"Just call me when you reach Miami, okay?"

"Okay. Goodbye."

"Hannah, wait!"

"What?" I asked, bringing the phone close my ear again.

"Feel free to *misbehave*," he said, laughing then hung up.

I shook my head. I couldn't even begin to imagine what was waiting for me when I got to Miami. I knew Patrick wasn't going to let it go. I never should have told him about me drunk kissing my bodyguard, but it was too late for that.

Patrick and I both lost our virginity when we were seniors in high school. Not with each other, of course. We didn't plan it. It just sort of happened. I gave my virginity to my then boyfriend, whom I loved and thought I was going to be with forever. Obviously, it didn't go that way. He dumped me a few weeks later. By then, it was too late for regrets. Sometimes I wished I would have waited for someone special. Then again, I could obviously never tell if a guy really loved me. If I did, I would still have my virginity, and I would have saved myself a lot of heartbreak.

Maybe being a man whore was the answer and Patrick had it all figured out.

The door suddenly opened and Nathan walked in, looking fresh himself. His hair was wet, making it look darker and he was wearing a perfectly clean black suit. I wondered how he cleaned off the dirt.

"The princess is awake," he said with a smile.

45

"Is the car here?" I asked as I began to put everything back in my suitcase. It was really messy in there, but I didn't have the patience to fold everything neatly. I'll just wash everything when I got to Patrick's.

"Yes," he said, swinging the keys in the air.

"Great," I said, zipping the suitcase. "Let's go."

We got the suitcases and headed out. Nathan checked out while I went outside. It was sunny today, but it was still cold. I could see people putting gas at the gas station, some were going into the diner we went in yesterday.

I spotted a black Cadillac car, a replica of the one we had, and headed to it. Nathan half-ran to open the back door for me, but I opened the passenger door.

He frowned at me.

"What?" I asked with a smile. "We're friends now, right? So I get to ride shotgun."

He shut the door and smiled. "Okay."

I turned on the radio as Nathan put on his seatbelt. "You brought chips," I said happily when I spotted a bag full of chips and candy in the backseat. I reached for it and took out a bag of Doritos and began to eat.

"As much as I would like for you to eat me, Hungry Hannah is much scarier."

I felt my face grow hot which made him chuckle.

I looked out the window as he began to drive. There were so many trees. I loved how they all looked lined up. For the first time in a long time, I felt completely normal. If we ignored the fact that Nathan was here as my bodyguard, I was just a regular person going on a road trip. No one knew where I was. No TV making up gossips about my family. No magazines I could get a glimpse of.

I took out my phone and called Rachel.

"How's Nick?" I asked right after she answered.

"Nicholas is great!" she sounded happy. "He opened his eyes this morning. He does have to stay in bed until he is

46

completely healed. He is being a pain in the ass because he doesn't like that but don't worry, I'll make sure he follows the instructions."

I laughed. "Yeah, sounds like him."

"What about you?" she asked. "Richard told me you were in a car accident?"

"I'm fine. It was nothing."

"I'm glad you're okay." She paused. "How are you, really? I know you've had to spend all this time with Nathan."

Rachel knew about the kiss with Nathan. I really should have kept my mouth shut. Now everyone was worried about it.

"Uh, yes," I said slowly, shifting uncomfortably on my seat. I casually turned down the volume of my phone so Nathan wouldn't hear what Rachel was telling me.

"He's there isn't he?"

"Yes…" I said awkwardly.

Rachel laughed. "I'm sorry, Hannah. I don't mean to make you uncomfortable. I just—I know that you say you are done with guys but I want you to know that it's okay to…you know…have fun."

"Rachel!" I hissed, laughing. God, she was the second person to tell me it's okay to mess around with my bodyguard. *What in the world was going on?*

She laughed again. "Your brother would kill me if he knew I was telling you this!" She sighed. "I just want you to be happy."

"Well, thank you," I said sarcastically. "I got to go. Keep me posted, will you?"

"Of course. Take care, Hannah."

"Nick okay?" Nathan asked after I hung up.

"Yes," I sighed. "Thank God."

"Is Mrs. Collins worried about me?" he asked after a moment.

I rolled my eyes at him. "Her name is Rachel."

"The last time I called her Rachel your brother almost took my eyes out."

47

I smiled. "Well, Rachel isn't like my brother. And no, she actually gave me her blessing to seduce you."

He raised his eyebrows, a smile was playing on his lips. "Really?"

"Yeah. I told her she didn't have to worry because we're just friends." I smiled, enjoying this.

"Friends who kiss."

My palms suddenly feel sweaty, and I ran them over my jeans. "Are you flirting with me?"

"Is it working?" he asked, glancing at me for a moment.

"Not really," I teased him. "You don't have game."

"Oh, believe me, Collins, I do. You're just not my type."

Ouch.

"Yeah, well, annoying bodyguards aren't my type either."

I didn't care that he said that.

I didn't care.

I didn't care.

I didn't care.

"We'll be good friends, then," he said with a smirk.

I didn't care.

"Yes, we will," I said, looking out the window.

Dammit. I did care.

CHAPTER 9

The next few hours went by really fast. We were quiet for most of the way, but it was a comfortable silence. Which of course, scared me. Everything about Nathan scared me. I knew I was starting to like him and there was nothing I could do about it.

"What did you do before you were a bodyguard?" I asked him as night began to fall on us.

A dark shadow crossed over Nathan's handsome face. "I was in the military."

"You were?" I asked in shock. At the same time, that explained his fire-making skills, the way he wouldn't sleep, how well his body was built. "How old are you?"

He chuckled, but I could hear a strain in it. I could tell he didn't like talking about this. I didn't blame him. "I am twenty-four. I joined when I was 18 and graduated from high school."

"You wanted to follow in your dad's footsteps." I realized.

He nodded slowly, looking straight ahead. "I did, yes. My mother was never okay with it, then again she was never okay with anything I did."

I smiled sadly. "Believe it or not, I know exactly how that feels."

He shrugged. "I don't really talk about this with anyone..."

"Because you don't have any friends?" I teased, trying to lighten up the mood. As much as I didn't want to admit it, I liked it when Nathan was all happy and laughing. He made me feel good. He was optimistic and I was starting to like it.

He laughed. "Pretty much, yes."

I looked out the window for a moment. "Is that why you don't sleep?" I really didn't want to push him but, at the same time, I couldn't seem to drop it. I wanted to know more about him.

I wasn't looking at him but, from the corner of my eye, I could see his hands grip the steering wheel. "I am just not used to sleeping, that's all."

I nodded slowly, knowing he was lying. "Okay."

I understood that he didn't like talking about it, but I couldn't help but worry about him. Not sleeping wasn't healthy and our bodies could only take so much. I wondered how bad his nightmares were.

I never pictured Nathan as a guy from the military. Maybe because of how happy he was all the time. Then I realized that, maybe he was just used to hiding his pain...hiding the fact that he couldn't sleep...

I bit my lip and leaned my head on the window. I stared at the trees outside until I fell asleep.

~

"...no, I told you I can't go...I'm working..."

It took me a moment to realize that Nathan was talking on the phone when I woke up. I kept my eyes closed and just sat there. I was curious about who he was talking to. Okay. I was eavesdropping. I was an eavesdropper now.

"...I just can't go..." He chuckled. "Jared—I really am working this time...I'm not even in New York...no, I can't tell you where I am."

The car came to a sudden stop.

"How many times have I told you that I don't want to go out with her again?" Nathan was arguing when I paid attention again. "I don't care, Jared. Call her and tell her it was all you. I don't like her that way. I am fine just being by myself." I could feel him looking at me and my heart began to beat faster.

Did he catch me? I decided it was time to wake up, so I opened my eyes slowly just to close them again. The sunlight coming through the windows made my eyes hurt. I realized it was morning and that we had stopped at a gas station.

"Listen, I got to go," Nathan said quickly. "Alright, bye." He turned the car off then turned to look at me. "Good morning."

I wiped my eyes with my hands. "Where are we?"

"I am hungry," he said, looking a little embarrassed.

"Hmm, me too," I murmured.

He laughed. "You literally just woke up."

"So?"

He just shook his head as he kept laughing. We got out of the car and I realized we were outside an iHop. The weather was not as cold as it was in New York. It was still cold, but a little less. The sun was really bright but it felt good as we made our way in.

I went to the restroom while Nathan ordered. I washed my face and brushed my teeth. For once, my hair actually seemed to agree with me so I let it down.

"So how far away is Miami now?" I asked when I got back to the table. The food wasn't there but the coffee was and I took a sip of it with a smile. I loved coffee.

"About 3 hours or less."

I sighed. "Good. I'm tired of living in the car."

"Nick is home by the way," Nathan said. "I spoke to your father," he explained when I looked at him.

Who else did you speak to?

I bit my tongue. It was really none of my business.

The server arrived with our food. I didn't think I would ever not be in the mood for pancakes. Or bacon. As she placed the plates in front of us, I studied Nathan. He hadn't slept for at least 24 hours and he didn't look as tired as he should. It wasn't normal…or healthy.

"That's good news," I said after the server left. "Do they know who did it yet?"

"No," he said with a frown.

"I wish I could help somehow."

51

He looked at me and half smiled. "You are helping. By staying safe."

I rolled my eyes at him. "What's going to happen? And if my death is in store, then it's going to happen whether I'm in New York or Miami or across the country."

"And you believe that everything happens for a reason."

I nodded as I put a forkful of pancake in my mouth. "I do."

He eyed me closely. "And you and I being here, do you think that's destiny?"

I looked up and met his green eyes. "I believe that every choice we've made, everything we do, we did because it was already written on stone somewhere. We are where we are supposed to be."

"So you kissing me, that was written on stone… somewhere," he said, a smile playing on his lips.

I rolled my eyes again. "You are never going to let me forget that, are you?"

"I never forget stolen kisses."

"Oh so now, I'm in debt with you or something?" I couldn't help but smile.

"Yes, you are." He leaned across the table, getting closer to me. "And believe me when I tell you that no one steals a kiss from me and gets away with it. I will be getting my kiss back."

I gulped.

He was flirting with me.

Oh.

My.

God.

He was flirting with me.

Or was he just playing? Was that the same thing? Was it sad that I couldn't tell if a guy was flirting or playing? Did I even know what flirting was? God, I sucked at this.

While I was having my mental panic attack, Nathan suddenly leaned in and, for a split second, I thought he was going to kiss me. I felt our lips brush as he moved to the corner of my

52

mouth and placed his lips against my skin. I felt him slide his tongue slowly and then he backed away.

I sat there, feeling something inside of me tingle.

"You had syrup," he said casually as he looked down at his food.

I sat there in shock, I could still feel his tongue on my skin…he had turned something on in me. That was so inappropriate, yet I found myself wanting more.

My cell phone began to ring then, making me jump. I picked it up, grateful for the distraction.

"Hello?" I answered, my voice still shaky. Nathan glanced at me with a smile.

"Is this Hannah Collins?" a raspy voice asked.

"Uh—who is this?" I asked and Nathan's face changed in an instant.

"Hannah Collins?" the voice asked again.

I stared at Nathan, not knowing what to say. He reached out and took the phone from my hand. "Who the hell is this?" he demanded angrily. After a moment, he hung up and then he took my phone and threw it to the floor with force.

I heard it crack, or maybe it was my heart too.

He stood up and stepped on it until the screen turned black. Then he took out his wallet and placed money on the table and reached for my hand.

"Come on, we need to go," he said, pulling me up.

"You—*m-my phone!*" I complained as he pulled me out of the restaurant.

His grip was strong and he was angry when he looked at me. I had never seen him like this. "Whoever that was, knows we are here. Now, do you want to sit here and cry over a broken phone or are you going to make me carry you into the car."

I narrowed my eyes at him. "I'll walk," I said in a small voice.

He didn't let my arm go as we walk back to the car.

I let him open the door for me as I still felt the sensations of his tongue on my skin.

CHAPTER 10

The ride to Miami was quick after that. I was exhausted like I had never been in my life. My whole body ached; I couldn't find a comfortable position in the seat. Nathan was right. It took about 3 hours to reach Miami. I borrowed Nathan's phone and texted Patrick to let him know we were going to be there soon. I had never been to Miami. Patrick was the one who always went to visit me in New York. Miami was beautiful and sunny, though it was winter so it wasn't hot. Something that I was grateful for.

Patrick lived in a condo, right in front of the beach. It was a really expensive condo his parents had bought him when he moved here. His parents were lawyers that lived in New York, Patrick rarely saw them. I think that the lack of attention from his parents was what made Patrick look for love somewhere else. Or, like he liked to call it, "good times." Though he didn't like talking about it which was another indication of the issue.

The condo was beautiful. I especially loved the clear glass that faced the side of the beach. I had seen the view from when we would Facetime and it looked unreal. Now, I couldn't wait to look out from the inside.

Nathan parked, and I smiled when I saw Patrick walking toward us.

Patrick was a very attractive guy. He had short blond hair with cute curls on top of his head and two bright blue eyes. He had a toned body that only spelled TROUBLE. It had been a long time since I had seen him and I jumped out of the car and half ran to him.

"Hannah!" he yelled, putting his arms around me, squeezing me.

"Ow," I complained when I heard my back crack.

He pulled back and scanned my body with his blue eyes. "You look horrible."

I laughed. "Thank you. I love the honesty."

He chuckled. "Right. Come on, I have your room ready," he said, putting an arm around my shoulders as he led me in. Nathan followed us, strangely quiet, with the suitcases and his duffel bag.

The condo reminded me of a dorm room in a novella I watched once but couldn't remember the name. It was small but it had two floors. Patrick showed me the living room and kitchen; the guest room and the laundry room were all downstairs.

I threw myself on the couch, face down, resting my forehead on my arm.

"Uh, Hannah, I have a room for you upstairs," Patrick said as he kneeled in front of me.

"No, no stairs, please. I'm good here," I murmured and then closed my eyes and had the best sleep I've had in days.

~

I woke up the next morning in a room I didn't remember coming to, but I figured Patrick carried me or something. The room was smaller than my room back home, but I didn't mind. There was a TV, two drawers, and a closet. My favorite part was the big window that faced the beach.

I got in the shower and changed into jeans with a blue blouse. I brushed my teeth and then made my way down the stairs. I could hear the sound of the TV in the background. Patrick was at the dining room table with an omelet in front of him. It was then that I realized he had a maid; she was cooking and smiled at me when she saw me. Patrick was on the phone when I took a seat in front of him.

He smiled at me then raised his index finger. "Listen, I got to go, but I'll call you later, okay?" he said. "Yeah, bye." He grinned at me. "You're finally awake."

The maid placed an omelet in front of me. "Thanks," I said and she just nodded.

"It's so beautiful here," I said as we ate. I looked around. "Where's Nathan?"

"Your bodyguard? He's been outside since last night. I told him he could have the guest room, but he refused. What's up with him?"

I looked down. "He just takes his job seriously."

Patrick placed his hand on top of mine. "You have no idea how happy I am that you're here. I missed you a lot, Hannah Banana."

I laughed. "Me too, Pat. I'm happy to be here with you."

"How's Nick?"

"He's good," I said, taking a sip of the orange juice. "What have you been up to?"

He shrugged. "Finished school, happy to be on break," he said, winking at me. He studied me for a moment. "You look good. How are you?"

"Good. I'm still sore from spending so much time in the car but good."

"Hannah," he said giving me that look.

I knew that wasn't what he meant but I hoped.

I sighed. "I'm okay, really. I think I'm over him."

"You think?" He raised his eyebrow. "God, I still want to go kick his stupid ass."

I rolled my eyes at him. "It's fine. Just another jerk added to the list."

He grinned at me. "Does your bodyguard have anything to do with you being over him?"

"Of course not," I said quickly. "We spent hours together in a car, Patrick, it was impossible to not become friends."

"So you guys are friends now…" he teased.

57

I rolled my eyes at him. "I'm starting to regret coming here," I joked.

"Hannah, come on. You can't lie to me. I know you like him."

I gulped. "Maybe a little."

He laughed. "Yeah, right. *A little.*"

I sighed. "So have you found the girl yet?" I asked, trying to change the subject.

He frowned. "What girl?"

"You know, the girl who is different from the others. The girl you're going to fall in love with and change you from your filthy ways," I said dramatically.

He laughed. "No such thing will happen."

"Sure," I told him with a smile.

"Not anytime soon. I'm too busy enjoying girls. Do you know how easy it is for me now to get them in my bed? I've gotten girls to take *me* to *their* place."

I shook my head. "You're a jerk," I said, standing up.

"Where are you going?"

"Nathan needs to eat," I said, making my way towards the front door.

"Aw, you already look after him like a good wifey."

I threw a pillow at him and then walked outside. I found Nathan leaning against the wall, facing the beach. He had his jacket off and had the sleeves of his shirt rolled up to his shoulders. I couldn't help but notice how the fabric hugged his broad shoulders and muscular arms. He had his foot behind him, resting on the wall, giving him that bad boy look. The sun was hitting his skin, making him look even more handsome.

He turned to look at me when he noticed that I was walking towards him. "You're awake," he stated.

"And so are you, *still.*"

"I'm okay," he assured me.

"You need to sleep," I told him.

"I did sleep."

"For how long?"

"Long enough," he said.

"You don't have to be outside, you know."

He shrugged. "I'm here to protect you, Hannah."

"Just come inside and eat."

He stood up in front of me and I suddenly felt correlated as I leaned my back against the wall and he walked closer. "I can't go inside."

"Why not?" I whispered.

It was so easy for him to make me nervous. It was embarrassing. I could already feel the tingles in my stomach by how close he was to me.

He placed a hand on the left side of my head, resting his palm against the wall. He clenched his jaw. "I *can't* stand seeing you with him," he said in a low voice.

"He's just my friend," I said, looking into his green eyes.

Where had this Nathan come from? I had never seen him so—determined? Angry? Possessive?

"I don't care who he is." He raised his hand and touched the side of my jaw with his finger, sending chills all over my body. "I *can't stand* to see him touch you."

"Nathan—" I whispered.

Oh god. It surprised me how much I liked to see this side of him. It made him even more sexy.

He placed his index finger on my lips, silencing me. "Keep your distance from him." He clenched his jaw. "*Please.*"

I gulped and then I nodded. "Okay."

He didn't move and just kept looking at me.

"Just come inside and eat something," I said, breaking the silence.

He finally took a step back and I took a deep breath. *Why had that turned me on? Why did it feel good?*

He was being *possessive* and I liked it.

"I'm serious, Hannah," he warned behind me as we made our way back inside.

"I know," I said but I was smiling.
This was a game I could play.

CHAPTER 11

When we were sixteen years old, Patrick and I decided to test our romantic potential. Everyone at school would always tell us that we would make a cute couple and that best friends fell in love all the time. I don't know, I think it was all the peer pressure that made us think it could work between us. When we tried to kiss, it was so awkward we burst out laughing and we knew right there, that we would never work. We were meant to be friends. Knowing that only made us get closer and we became more comfortable with each other.

No one understood our friendship like we did.

At least, Nathan obviously didn't.

As we made our way back into the condo, I felt flushed. I didn't know what was wrong with me. Nathan and I weren't anything. He wasn't my boyfriend. He didn't have the right to demand anything from me.

At the same time, I knew that we were *something*.

We had been flirting our way here.

I decided I would play his game or whatever it was because I was really enjoying it so far.

"You're back—great," Patrick said when we walked back inside.

I nodded. "Yeah."

I took a seat and Nathan sat next to me. There was already a plate for him. He was quiet. It almost made me want to laugh. I had never seen him so serious.

"I was thinking we could go out," Patrick began as we resumed our breakfast.

"Right now?"

"Yeah, why not? I could take you to the mall, you know just in case you needed to buy something for tonight."

I frowned. "What's tonight?"

"Beach party."

"I don't know, Patrick. You know I don't really like parties."

"You're coming," he stated.

What was it with everyone wanting to boss me around?

I remembered that I did need a new phone so I agreed to go to the mall. So an hour later, Nathan was pulling into the mall parking lot with Patrick and I in the back seat.

"So this is what it feels like to be famous," Patrick said, nodding.

I rolled my eyes at him. "You're exaggerating."

"No, really. Does he—" he pointed at Nathan's back, "—do everything you tell him to?"

I raised my eyebrows. "You would be surprised."

I thought I saw Nathan smile after I said that. We got out of the car and then walked into the mall, which looked like any other mall. All the malls looked the same to me. We went into the first clothing store we saw. I began to look through the clothes while Nathan stayed close to me.

"Hannah."

I looked up from the dress I was looking at to Patrick who was wiggling a really short skirt with a smirk. "No," I told him.

"Why not?" he asked walking towards me.

"It's too short—I already don't like showing my legs."

"Hannah, don't be ridiculous. You are hot," Patrick told me and I felt Nathan's body tense next to me.

I rolled my eyes at him. "I'm not wearing that," I said taking a step back, bumping into Nathan. *Why was he always standing so close?* I held on to his jacket to keep myself from falling and then I feel something hard on his waistline. I pulled his jacket open and felt my eyes get wide.

"Since when do you carry a gun?" I whispered.

"Your father asked me to. It's no big deal," he said looking amused.

I bit my lip as I turned around and went back to looking at some dresses. I thought maybe my dad and Nathan were hiding something from me. Maybe this was more serious than I thought.

I grabbed a black dress and made my way to the fitting rooms. Patrick followed me but Nathan stopped him with a hand on his shoulder.

Patrick turned to look at him. "What the hell is your problem?"

"She goes in *alone*," Nathan told him in a low voice.

Patrick turned to look at me. "Is he serious?"

"Just wait here," I told Patrick and then shut the door.

I tried on the black dress, which reached me down below mid-thigh. All the dresses seemed a good idea until I tried them on. I didn't know why I didn't like showing my legs. It had always been an insecurity of mine. I walked out of the fitting room. "Let's go," I said as I made my way out.

"Do I have permission to get a phone?" I teased Nathan as we stopped by a cellphone store.

There was a smile playing on his lips. "You may."

I smiled. "Thank you."

Nathan stayed outside the store because he received a call, so Patrick and I went in.

"You flirt with him!" Patrick chuckled. "You want him, don't you? Oh, you want him so badly."

"Shh!" I hissed. "I just like teasing him." I laughed. "Shut up."

"I'm not saying it's a bad thing," Patrick said grinning at me. "I mean, no homo but he's an attractive fellow."

I laughed. "Stop it, I'm getting jealous."

He smiled. "You should have some fun. Seriously, Hannah, when was the last time you had sex? Have you even had sex after high school?"

"That's none of your business!" I hissed as we waited to be helped.

"I just want you to have fun. You know, loosen up." He winked at me.

"So you're telling me I should sleep with my bodyguard."

"If you feel nothing but attraction for him, yes." He frowned. "Hannah?"

"What?" I asked looking away.

"Can you look at me in the eye and tell me you haven't fallen for him?" Patrick asked, placing his hands on my shoulders.

From behind him, I saw Nathan began to make his way into the store. How could someone not fall for him? He was so manly, so handsome, so caring, so kind...

Thankfully, Patrick's phone began to ring then, making his hands drop to get it. He frowned at the caller ID.

"One of your ladies?" I asked him.

"What is it with girls thinking one-night stands can mean more than one-night stands?" Patrick said as Nathan joined us. He stood next to me.

"You're an ass," I told him with a disapproval look.

He shrugged. "I am always honest with them. I always tell them it's just a one-time thing, yet they still call me the next morning."

I shook my head at him. "I wish you wouldn't do that, Pat."

He frowned at me. "Don't give me that look."

"I just don't understand why guys have to be assholes."

Patrick looked at Nathan. "She just insulted us."

Nathan actually chuckled.

"I'm being serious," I insisted.

At that time, someone finally came over and helped us. The phone was taken out under Nathan's name since he didn't think it was safe to do it under mine. The paperwork was really boring so I was glad when we were finally done.

"You know it's good that your bodyguard drives," Patrick said as we made our way back to the car. "He'll be our designated driver tonight."

"I'm not drinking," I said.

"Yes, you are," Patrick said, confidently.

I glanced at Nathan as he opened the door for me. He smiled, as if he knew what I was thinking. The last time I got drunk I kissed him. I didn't want that to happen again, right?

When we got back to the condo, Patrick said he was "going to pay a friend a visit" which was code for "going to go get laid" and he left after making me promise I would be ready by eight.

I went up to my room and Nathan followed me, leaning on the doorway and crossing his arms on his chest. "I don't see it."

"What?" I asked, looking up at him as I placed the bags on the floor.

"I don't understand how he's your best friend."

"He wasn't always this crazy," I assured him. I frowned at the bags that were starting to form under his eyes. "You're starting to look like me during finals week. You need to sleep."

He shook his head but a yawn betrayed him.

"You could sleep here, Nathan. You don't have to sleep alone," I reached for his hand and pulled him to the bed.

I thought he really was tired because he didn't protest. He lay on the bed and stared up at the ceiling. "I don't always have nightmares," he whispered as I sat down next to him on the bed. It sounded like he was trying to convince himself that it was a good idea to sleep.

"And if you do it's fine. Just sleep, please," I said turning off the light.

It was still early, around two in the afternoon, so the sunlight was still coming through the window but it didn't seem to bother him because he shut his eyes and he fell into a soundless sleep.

I reached out and pulled his hair back. He looked so peaceful as he slept. I reached and pulled the blanket over him.

He didn't do more than shuffle in the bed but he didn't wake up.

I wondered if that was a good sleep for him.

I wondered what his worst nights looked like.

I knew I wasn't supposed to care so much about him.

The thing was: I did.

CHAPTER 12

I dug my toes into the soft sand as I stared at the beach. It was so beautiful. I loved the sound of the waves crashing against each other. The sand and water were cold but they felt good at the same time. I had jeans on with a hoodie and my Vans. I knew I wasn't dressed for a party but I didn't care.

The party was a few feet away from where I was. It was a few houses down from Patrick's condo. The music was too loud to even make out the words and the house was super crowded. People were drinking and kissing and doing other things that made me look away when I realized what they were doing. I hadn't even gone in the house and Patrick was too busy with girls to make me go inside with him.

I left Nathan sleeping in my bed. I didn't have the heart to wake him up. I needed him to sleep. He deserved it. Besides, I wasn't that far from the condo and it was too dark for people to even notice me. Except for some guy, Cesar, who had followed me out to the beach.

He was tall with a slim body and was wearing shorts with a shirt and sweater. He had short brown hair and brown eyes. He seemed nice but I wished he would leave me alone. I just wanted to enjoy the beach. He was standing next to me and I looked around us nervously. He was standing too close for my liking. I didn't even know the guy. I just met him a few minutes ago. He introduced himself as "Patrick's boy" which was weird.

"You're not a party girl, are you?" Cesar said as he took a sip of the beer in his hand.

"Not really," I said, not even looking at him, hoping he would get the message and leave me alone.

"The beach is something, huh?" he asked, nodding towards it.

"Yes, it's beautiful," I murmured.

He turned to look at me. "Not as beautiful as you."

I smiled at him. "Thank you."

He looked down at my lips and I took a step back. "Cesar—" His mouth was suddenly on my lips and I put my hands on his chest and tried to push him away. "Cesar—stop!" I yelled pushing him.

He took a step back.

"What? I thought you wanted to have some fun?" he asked with a smirk. His breath reeked of beer.

I glared at him. "No, I don't."

He suddenly reached for me and put his arm around my shoulders.

"Let me go!" I protested but he ignored me. The people around us were either too drunk or thet simply didn't care to help me.

"Let her go!" I heard Nathan yell behind me. He pushed Cesar off, sending him flying out to the sand.

Nathan took a step forward but I grabbed his arm.

"That's enough." I looked up at him. "Thank you."

Nathan turned his glare to me. "You should have woken me up," he told me in disapproval. His breath smelled like mint and I knew he had brushed his teeth. He must have barely woken up.

"I didn't want to wake you. You needed sleep."

"I need to protect you," he insisted.

I rolled my eyes at him. "Thank you but it was just some stupid drunk guy, Nathan." I glanced at Cesar who was still on the ground. *He wasn't dead, right?* No. I saw him groan as he moved to the side.

Nathan's green eyes softened as he turned to look at me. "You're not allowed to kiss anyone but me when you're drunk, okay?"

The butterflies in my stomach made me smile at him. I hated that I loved the feeling. I hated that I loved what he said to me. "Yes, sir," I said then turned around and began to walk on the edge of the beach, away from the stupid party.

"Did you sleep okay?" I asked him as we walked.

"I did." He frowned. "Did you try to seduce me in my sleep?"

"What? No." I laughed. Touching his face didn't count as seducing right?

"If you want to seduce me, I'd prefer it if you did it while I'm wide awake." He winked at me.

"You know you're not supposed to flirt with me right?"

He looked at me. "I think you broke that rule the moment you kissed me."

I smiled. "So it's my fault now."

He shrugged. "You did do it…"

"Fine but don't blame me when they fire you because of me."

"That depends…"

I looked up at him. "On what?"

He grinned at me. "On how far you are going to let me go."

I shook my head with a smile. "Why are you always flirting with me?"

"It happens to be my favorite part of the day," he teased.

"Why do you do it?"

He shrugged. "It's just flirting, Hannah. I'm not asking you to marry me," he said softly then raised his eyebrow. "Unless you want me to stop?"

I rolled my eyes at him. "I don't," I said, feeling a little embarrassed.

He smiled. "You know, you think you have the worst luck when it comes to relationships, you haven't stopped to think how, maybe, you aren't the problem."

"It wasn't just one heartbreak, it was a few," I reminded him then shrugged. "I don't believe that every guy is a jerk. I just don't trust my judgment anymore." I turned to look at him. "Have you ever had girlfriends?"

"I have."

"And?"

He shrugged. "I guess you can say I didn't have the best judgment either," he said, smiling at me.

I laughed. "Are you making fun of me?"

"I'm not." He smiled. "We've all had bad relationships, Hannah, that doesn't mean that it was a lack of judgment. It means it wasn't meant to be, that's it. Weren't you the one who said you believed we all are where we are supposed to be?" He shrugged. "You need to stop putting yourself down so much and just *live*."

I didn't know what to think. Nathan was something else. And he was different when we were alone. I thought back to earlier...

I looked away. "You know, earlier you told me to stay away from Patrick..."

"Yes," he said slowly, looking at his feet as we walked.

I glanced at him. "What makes you think you can tell me what to do?"

"I didn't."

"Yes, you did."

"I told you I didn't stand it when he touched you," he said looking straight ahead.

"Right."

"I was just letting you know in case..."

I looked at him. "In case?"

He met my gaze. "In case I broke his jaw."

I shook my head with a smile to hide my how flattered I felt. "Why would you do that?"

We had stopped walking by then and Nathan reached out and wrapped his arm around my waist, pulling me closer to him. His move was unexpected but so smooth, as if he did that all the time. It made my heart flutter. I loved the feeling of his arm around my waist. It felt intimate. I felt protected.

"I can't stand it when someone else touches you," he said in a low voice. "I want it to be *just me*."

I looked down at his chest, sheepishly.

No one had ever said that to me before. That was the thing about Nathan—he said the most unexpected, most perfect things. He said things that made my knees feel weak. Things that made me want to forget about stupid standards and just kiss him like I did that night.

He reached down and pulled my chin up so I was forced to look at him. "You are so beautiful, Hannah." He looked into my eyes. "You don't know how beautiful you are to me." His eyes slowly began to drift down my nose, and then down my lips. It was then when he whispered, "I want to kiss you…"

71

CHAPTER 13

NATHAN

The first Collins I met was Christina Collins, Richard's wife. From what I knew, she was the one that took care of hiring the "service people," as she called it. The first thing I learned from her was that she was a very strict, conceited woman. I didn't expect anything else. I had worked with wealthy families before so I had some experience in working with those type of people. I didn't blame her. It must be hard not to become arrogant when you had so much money.

"You must always remember that you are here to do your job and nothing else," she had told me that day as I sat on the chair inside her husband's office. She walked in circles around me as if waiting for me to do something inappropriate. I could tell she wanted to intimidate me.

I nodded. "Of course, ma'am."

"You will be under my watch for the first few weeks, don't think your job is secure here." She gave me a hard look with her blue eyes. "I will be watching."

I didn't know what to say so I just nodded again. I was assigned to be her bodyguard for that week and it wasn't as bad as it could have been. She tried to make my life impossible by giving me endless orders, sometimes I felt more like a slave than a bodyguard. But I had worked with her type so I was able to surpass it and just hoped they would assign me to another family member.

In that first week, I met Nick Collins and his wife, Rachel who was the most humble, at least to the employees. She even cooked for everyone sometimes. She had always been really nice. I

72

also met Derek once. It wasn't really a meet-and-greet since I just saw him walk into a car. Word was that he was always traveling and that he was going to live in Paris for the time being. I also met Colton, who lived in the mansion with everyone else back then. He was engaged and seemed very happy with his fiancée.

On a Sunday, exactly a week after my first day, I was called into the office by Mr. Richard Collins himself. To say I was nervous was an understatement. Who wouldn't get nervous when you get called into your boss's office? Richard was a big, highly regarded man. He was sitting behind the desk with a laptop opened in front of him and talking on the phone when I walked in. He was busy promoting his new movie back then so I hadn't met him until that day.

I was standing up with my hands clasped in front of me, waiting.

"Sorry about that," Richard said as he hung up. "It's Nathan, right?"

I nodded.

"Please take a seat," he said, waving to the chair in front of him. I took a seat and waited for him to continue. "Word is that you were in the army, is that correct?"

I had not put that in my resume so I was quite surprised when he mentioned that. I guess they really did the whole background check really well. I nodded. "Yes, sir."
He smiled, a warm smile you wouldn't expect from such a powerful man. "My respect goes to you."

I nodded. "Thank you, sir."

He looked at me, thoughtfully. "I have a daughter, my youngest, have you met her?"

I shook my head. "No, sir."

"Hannah." He smiled. "She is my baby girl, my most beautiful treasure. I don't know what I would do if something were to happen to her. Do you understand?"

I half smiled. I understood where this was going. "Yes, sir."

73

"I want you to be her personal bodyguard." He sighed. "There have been some weird things going on and I worry about her safety. I know I can't do anything about people following her around but I can enforce her safety. I believe that you are suitable for the job. Am I wrong to believe so?" He studied me with his brown eyes.

I shook my head. "No, sir. My sole interest is to keep your family safe."

"From now on, your interest will be to keep *Hannah* safe. You will not leave her side. You do anything to keep her safe, do you understand?"

"I do."

He smiled at me. "I knew you are my guy. Now, she is outside in the garden. Why don't you go meet her?" he said as he opened the computer in front of him. I was dismissed thereafter.

"Of course."

"Thank you."

I nodded at him before walking out the door. As I was walking out, I realized that I had no idea how old Hannah was. *Was she a little girl? What if she was a little rebel?* I decided that it didn't matter who she was. She was my responsibility starting that day.

"Nathan!"

I stopped and turned around. Robin, the head of bodyguards and also my friend, walked toward me. "What happened? You in trouble?"

I shook my head. "No. He assigned me to his daughter. Hannah? Do you know her?"

He nodded with a smile as if remembering something pleasant. "Of course, I know her. She is a really sweet girl. You have nothing to worry about."

I sighed in relief. "Alright. That's good. I'm gonna go find her."

"Alright, man."

I headed outside where it was cold and it made me wonder why she would be outside with this weather. I found her sitting under a tree with a blanket underneath her. She had her knees up where she had a sketch book. She had a pencil in her right hand and she was drawing something. She had long, wavy brown hair and fair skin. She was wearing jeans with an oversized sweater. She looked comfy.

As I walked up to her, I was hesitant to interrupt what she was doing. She looked concentrated in whatever she was writing, but before I could turn around, she looked up at me with a confused look on her pretty face. She looked between eighteen and nineteen.

"Hello," I said then cleared my throat. "I am Nathan."

She smiled at me and I immediately saw the resemblance between her and her father. She looked nothing like her mom, not in appearance and not in the way she treated people. I knew that instantly.Hannah wouldn't be as receptive of service people.

"Hello, Nathan."

I smiled. "Your father he, um—"

She nodded. "He told me. I appreciate you coming to meet me but I'm not going out today so you can do something else."

I took a step forward. "I have strict instructions to not leave your side. So I will stay here, with you."

She shrugged. "Suit yourself." She went back to her sketching.

I leaned against the tree, behind her. She had a bag of Doritos, a water bottle, and some other pencils. I looked over her shoulder and realized that she was designing a dress or at least that's what it looked like. This girl could draw. She had a ring on her fourth finger and I wondered if she had a boyfriend. Then I stopped thinking about that because that was none of my business, unless he was an abusive boyfriend who posed a threat to her.

As I got to know Hannah, I was astonished by how amazing she was. She was so unlike all the other people I've worked for. I had protected other people because it was simply my job but Hannah—I actually *wanted* to protect her. We didn't really talk that much. Most of the things I had learned and knew about her was by being there with her all the time, observing and watching her.

She was a calm girl who loved coffee and reading. She laughed about everything—that was just who she was. And she always had a book in her hand. Romance books. Lots and lots of books.

I found her fascinating. She was so passionate about what she liked and that was proven when she asked out the guy she liked. It bothered me when she started dating him. Not because I was jealous or anything but because she was the one who always initiated their dates. It bothered me because she deserved so much more but she was too in love to see it.

I never said a word.

I had enough experience in this job to know better than get in somebody else's business. I was just her bodyguard. I was just there to protect her. Knowing what happened in her life was just a bonus.

Seeing her cry for him moved something in me. I could see the pain she was in just by looking at her. One day, about two weeks after they broke up, I was driving her back to her house when she had suddenly started crying again. It was so painful to watch. I parked the car and just waited in silence until she stopped crying. I looked out the window and cursed the idiot who hurt her in my head. I was so angry. I wanted to hurt him.

I knew it wasn't appropriate for me to care so much for my boss's daughter. It bothered me how much I noticed and cared about her. It wasn't right. I wanted to ask her if she was alright but I forced myself to keep my poker face and look straight ahead at the road in front of me.

It was the night after that when she kissed me in that bar after having a few drinks. I was surprised when she did it. I didn't get a warning. She simply turned to me and pressed her lips against mine. They were gentle and reminded me of a peach's soft skin. She tasted like vodka. I knew she was either not going to remember kissing me or she was going to regret it the next day. She was out of character.

Sure enough, the very next day I was told that I wasn't on her service anymore. I shrugged it off, half expecting it after the kiss last night. Hannah began to pretend that I didn't exist and I told myself I didn't give a damn. She was just a little immature girl unable of taking responsibility of her own actions and moving on. It had been just a kiss. What did she think was gonna happen? Did she think I had fallen in love with her? It bothered me that she made a big deal out of a simple kiss but it bothered me even more that I cared so much about not being on her service anymore.

It was an adjustment I had to go through. It was also new to me. Usually, I kept my distance from my protégées. I had learned my lesson the hard way from my previous job about what happens when you let your guard down. This was a job. An assignment. That was it...at least that was what I kept telling myself. Hannah could ignore me all she wanted, it wasn't going to change anything...

Because what she didn't remember was that I didn't have a *single* drink that night and I *kissed her back*.

CHAPTER 14

"I want to kiss you…" Nathan whispered, looking down at my lips.

I was utterly and completely enchanted by the charming guy in front of me. I found myself looking down at his full, perfect lips. Nathan wanted to kiss me.

Someone suddenly screamed somewhere from behind me, making me jump. I took a step back and turned around. A girl running away from a guy, laughing and screaming like a crazy person. No doubt that she was drunk.

"We should get back," I murmured then began walking back to the condo without waiting for him.

The walk back was awkward. Nathan didn't walk beside me but I could feel him close by. I just didn't understand why he would want to kiss me. *Did he like me? He couldn't like me. I was his boss's daughter. He had to know that he would lose his job if something ever happened between us.* I hated it when I did this. I always got ahead of myself. I always had the tendency to make something big out of something so little. Why couldn't I just let him kiss me? I knew I wanted him to. Why couldn't I stop fighting myself and do whatever I wanted?

The party was still going hard in the house as we walked back. I guess the later it got, the wilder people had become. I walked into the condo, feeling Nathan close behind. Inside, it was surprisingly quiet except for the faintest sound of the music coming from the party. As I reached the stairs, I thought Nathan had made his way to the guest room downstairs, until I felt his hand around my arm. He pulled me back down to him.

He smiled at me as his arm went around my waist again and he crashed his lips against mine, without giving me any warning. He did it so fast, I didn't even realize what was happening until we were already kissing. I felt his tongue slide over my lower lip, asking for permission. I opened my mouth, giving him access. I put my hand on the back of his neck and pressed myself closer to him.

I didn't remember his kiss being this good.

This ridiculously good.

I didn't know how long we kissed but I knew it was the longest I've been kissed. Before he pulled away, Nathan bit my lower lip. A small moan escaped my throat.

He looked at me, his eyes full of lust. "Don't walk away from me, Hannah, *ever*."

I didn't say anything. I was unable to look away and still trying to catch my breath. He let me go and turned around after that. I watched as he disappeared into his room. I stood there for a moment, still shaken from the kiss.

He can't just give me the best kiss of my life and walk away?

I licked my lips and realized they were a little swollen. I felt my face grow hot as I walked up the stairs quickly, barely feeling the steps underneath my feet.

I shut the door and leaned on it for a moment.

My heart was beating fast against my chest...and then I started laughing. The kiss was so great that I was laughing. I threw myself on the bed and buried my face in the pillow as I tried to gather my thoughts. Nathan had to be the hottest guy I had ever kissed. I couldn't stop thinking about him. I couldn't stop thinking about the kiss...about how good it felt to be in his arms.

The lust I could see in his eyes...

Never in my wildest dreams did I imagine someone as attractive as Nathan would like me.

I buried my face in the pillow but even that couldn't stop the big smile on my lips. I didn't fall asleep until very late that night, mostly because I couldn't stop thinking about Nathan.

When I woke up the next morning, I felt good. Lighter. Happier.

I got in the shower, brushed my teeth, did the things I did every morning with a smile on my face. The thought of seeing Nathan made me nervous, which made me want to eat food. I walked downstairs and headed straight for the fridge without looking at anything else.

"Well, look who's finally up," Patrick said behind me.

I looked up and realized that he was on the couch, watching TV. At the same time, Nathan walked in coming from the hallway. He was wearing his usual suit, looking handsome like always. I blushed when our eyes met. I looked away quickly.

Patrick frowned. "Are you alright?" he asked from the couch.

I gulped as I checked for anything in the fridge. "Uh— yeah. Just hungry," I murmured.

"Are you going to hide behind the fridge all day?"

I froze and realized that Nathan was right behind me, making my body feel tingly and shaky. I avoided his gaze as I reached for the mayo and ham.

I laughed nervously. "No." I walked to the kitchen counter then took out two slices of bread. I busied my hands by spreading the mayo slowly. I glanced at Patrick who was busy looking at his phone.

"Hannah…" Nathan said as he leaned against the counter.

"What?" I asked, putting the ham on the bread and then putting the other slice on top.

"Look at me," he demanded in a low voice.

"I'm eating," I said, biting the sandwich.

"Look at me," he repeated.

"Nathan told me what happened last night with Cesar," Patrick said as he walked into the kitchen.

Nathan took a step back, crossing his arms on his strong chest. I could feel his eyes on me but I ignored him as I chewed. "You know him?" I frowned as I remembered the jerk.

80

Patrick nodded. "Yeah, he's an asshole. I'll take care of him."

I rolled my eyes at him. "What is it with you guys wanting to fight? Does it feed your ego?" I asked, pointing at my head.

Patrick chuckled. "Woke up feisty today."

"And you need to stop drinking so much. It's a miracle your liver still works." I knew I was babbling. It was because I was nervous. I could feel Nathan watching me and my body responded to him.

"You're worse than my mom," Patrick said with a frown.

I shook my head at him. "Someone has to be the one to tell you."

He placed his hands on my shoulders. "Hannah."

"Patrick." I couldn't help but laugh as I mocked his tone.

"Are you bipolar or something? One moment you're all riled up and suddenly you're laughing," he remarked, looking confused.

I laughed then sighed. "I just worry about you."

He grinned. "I know, I like it."

"You're a child."

He laughed as he walked past me. "We are going to dinner tonight," he told me before he went upstairs.

As soon as Patrick was out of sight, Nathan took a step forward and stood in front of me.

"We need to talk," he said.

I looked at the floor. "No, we don't."

"I need you to look at me," he whispered, taking a step towards me.

"Nathan—"

"Look at me," he interrupted.

He was being so demanding. *Why was that so hot?*

I sighed but forced myself to look up and meet his gaze. His green eyes looked so intense as he looked into my eyes.

"I need to know if this is how you're going to act every time after I kissed you," he said softly. "Because if that's the case,

I'll have to stop and believe me, I don't want to," he said gazing at my lips.

"You realize that this is a bad idea, right?" I asked him.

There was a smile playing on his lips. "Is it?"

"Yes, a really, *really* bad idea."

His hand went up to my cheek and he began to stroke it with the back of his hand. "It doesn't feel that way."

I grabbed his hand to make him stop because his touch made my knees feel weak. "Do you want to keep kissing me?" I whispered.

"All the time…" he said, he was so close that I could feel his lips moved against mine as he spoke.

"You can't tell anyone about this…" I whispered, closing my eyes.

"About what?" he said, closing the gap between us. "It's just a kiss…"

CHAPTER 15

I rolled my eyes at the blank sketch of paper in front of me. I had been meaning to sketch something, get my mind off of things for a while but nothing was coming to me. The only thing I wanted to draw was how good Nathan looked on the beach. It had been a week since we arrived and Nathan and Patrick were actually been getting more along now. Today wasn't as cold as it had been so we decided to spend some time outside. Nathan and Patrick were throwing a football back and forth, joking and messing around.

I smiled as I watched them.

Nathan was actually wearing jeans with a red sweater and white T-shirt underneath. It was the first time I had seen him not wearing a suit. He looked like a college student as he played with Patrick. And of course, very good-looking.

"Hannah?"

"Huh?" I asked as I pressed the phone closer to my ear. I had forgotten that I was talking to Nick.

Nick chuckled. "I asked you how you were liking Miami so far."

I smiled. "Oh, it's great! I really like it here and I'm happy to spend some time with Patrick."

"I'm glad you're having a good time." He cleared his throat. "I wanted to talk to you about your bodyguard, Nathan?"

I frowned. "Uh—what about him?"

"Last time I checked, you hated him. Don't think I forgot when you asked Dad to take him off your service. I know you never wanted to tell me what he did to you—"

"He didn't do anything to me," I said quickly. Too quickly. I tried to think back and try to remember exactly how I told my dad I didn't want Nathan to be my bodyguard. Maybe I had been overly dramatic than I should.

"So you just hated him for no reason?"

"I didn't hate him."

"Listen, I just wanted to know if you're comfortable with him. I want to know if you feel safe with him…since I know you're stuck with him because of what happened to me…"

I looked up at Nathan who was just catching the ball from Patrick. He was shouting something at Patrick as he threw the ball back at him.

"What happened to you is not your fault." I smiled. "And, yes, Nickelodeon. I feel very safe with him."

Nick laughed. "Okay, I believe you."

"So how are you? How's Rachel?"

"I'm so tired of being in bed." He groaned. "Rachel is good. She doesn't let me do anything."

"She's just taking care of you."

"I know." I could almost see his smile.

"I can't believe you still don't know who shot you," I said quietly.

I had lost sleep a few nights trying to think about who could have done this to Nick. But I didn't know enough about the people who worked for him and his business partners. I had been meaning to talk to Rachel about it. She worked with Nick so she had to have an idea. I didn't like to admit it but the thought of someone wanting to hurt my family scared me.

"I know, it's ridiculous. I feel bad because Dad is working so hard and the media has been all over him. I had to force Rachel to take a bodyguard."

"She agreed?"

Rachel had always hated the idea of bodyguards. She always refused to have one.

"Not exactly. Let's just say I had guilt-jerked her into agreeing." He laughed.

"Well, I hope they'll catch whoever shot you before I have to go back to school."

Christmas was coming and I didn't mind spending it in Miami with Patrick but school was just something I couldn't miss, though. It was my last semester; there was no way I would let myself get behind.

"I know. We'll hopefully figure this whole thing out soon." He paused. "I'll call you later, Hannah, please take care. Let Nathan take care of you."

I smiled. "You too, Nick. Love you."

"Love you too, bye."

I hung up and stared at the blank piece of paper in front of me then shut the book. I didn't know what was happening to me. Usually, sketching helped take my mind off of things but today, I couldn't seem to be able to draw anything.

"Hey." I looked up and watched as Nathan took a seat next to me. He sat close enough that our arms were touching.

"Hey," I said looking for Patrick. He was talking with some girl. I rolled my eyes. "Patrick ditched you?"

He shrugged. "I don't mind."

"You seem to be getting along with him," I commented with a smile.

"He's okay, I guess." He turned to look at me. "I still don't like it when he's with you though."

I looked at him. "What's your problem? Patrick is my best friend. You make it sound like he touches me inappropriately or something."

"I know he's your friend. I just can't help it. I guess I get jealous," he said as he ran a hand through his soft-looking brown hair.

I bit my lower lip. "So am I just not supposed to have friends?"

"You can, as long as they don't get close to you." His eyes looked amused.

I shook my head. "Since when did you become so possessive?"

"Since I decided to accept the fact that I like you." He leaned in. "*A lot*," he whispered in my ear.

I just smiled, not knowing what to say. Then there was a moment of silence. I watched as Patrick and the girl headed into the bar by the beach. I sighed, enjoying the sound of the waves. It seemed to be the only thing that could relax me nowadays.

"Who were you talking to?" Nathan asked, breaking the silence between us.

"Why?" I asked him.

He shrugged. "Curious."

I smiled. "If I tell you, will you tell me who Jared is?"

He frowned at me. "How did you know about Jared?"

I looked at the waves of the ocean, feeling embarrassed. "I may have heard a conversation I wasn't supposed to hear—back in the car."

Nathan smiled. "I got myself an eavesdropper."

I rolled my eyes at him. "Like you don't listen to everything I say."

"It's my job."

"Exactly," I said, turning to him. "You know a lot about me. I know nothing about you. It's not fair."

"There is not really a lot to know," he said with a shrug.

"Who's Jared?"

"He's my friend. He likes to think he's my wingman."

"He arranges dates for you?"

"Once in a while, yes." He shook his head. "A few weeks ago, he arranged a blind date for me with some girl…"

"Did you like *her?*" I asked, trying to hide the fact that I didn't like the thought of Nathan with another girl. Maybe I understood how he felt about seeing me with Patrick…just a little.

86

"Not really. I don't really like blondes." He leaned in. "I'm more into brunettes."

I could feel his hot breath against my neck. "Oh really?"

"Yes, into sexy, beautiful brunettes," he said, placing his hand on my thigh.

Oh God.

I felt his lips on my cheek. He kissed me softly. I closed my eyes as I felt him linger on my chin, placing small kisses until he reached my mouth. He pressed his lips against mine and didn't move for a moment.

It felt so good.

I felt his hand go behind my neck as he kissed me. I leaned down until my back was against the cold sand but even that couldn't lower my temperature. Nathan leaned over me as he kissed me.

"My beautiful Hannah," he whispered against my lips.

I ran my hand through his hair as I looked up at him.

He smiled down at me. "What are you doing to me?"

I traced his face with my index finger, not wanting to talk. My brain and heart were saying two different things, and I didn't want to ruin the moment.

Instead, I pulled my head up and closed the gap between us.

CHAPTER 16

The next day, Patrick dragged me to go with him to an outlet mall. The amount of money Patrick spent on clothes was astonishing. Even I didn't spend that much money on my clothes. Patrick had always been a fashionable guy. He liked to look good.

"So besides wasting money on clothes you don't need, what else do you need to buy?" I asked as we walked. The mall was really packed as people were also buying gifts for the holidays. Nathan walked next to me.

"I met someone."

I turned to look at Patrick, mouth hanging open.

He laughed. "Just kidding. Last night I was watching TV and this commercial about online dating kept coming up and people in the ad kept saying 'I met someone.'" He shrugged. "Sorry I just wanted to say it."

"What does that have to do with anything?" I asked him, laughing.

"Nothing." He laughed. "Well, I'm actually on a mission," he said as we walked. "A girl said no to me last night."

"No way," I said sarcastically.

He narrowed his eyes at me. "You think this is a joke."

"I think that if someone says no, then it's no. What is it with guys wanting what they can't have?"

"Exactly! That's the problem. I've always had anyone I wanted." He winked at me. "Good thing that everyone has a price."

"I don't."

He raised an eyebrow at me. "So, you're telling me that if a billionaire comes and proposes to you, you'll say no?"

"Yes, I would say no."

Patrick threw an arm around my shoulders. "Would you marry *me*?"

"Why would I do that?" I said with a smile. I glanced at Nathan but he seemed amused by our conversation. I guessed Patrick didn't bother him anymore. But why was I disappointed? Maybe because I had always found his jealousy incredibly hot.

He shrugged. "You know, maybe if we're both 40 and single, we can get married. I don't want to see my best friend become a cat lady."

I laughed. "Thank you for being so thoughtful."

Patrick glanced at Nathan. "How about you, Nathan? Would you marry Hannah?"

I punched Patrick in the stomach making him let me go from his grasp. "*Patrick.*"

"What?" he asked innocently then looked at Nathan again. "Or do you not find Hannah attractive? Come on, we're in a circle of trust here."

I glared at Patrick. "I'm going to kill you," I mouthed at him.

Nathan turned to look at us with an amused expression on his face. "Circle of trust?"

"Yes, nothing here will get to the ears of Mr. Boss Collins, I promise," Patrick said with a big grin on his stupid face.

This was so not funny.

"Well, in that case," Nathan glanced at me, "I find Hannah *very* attractive."

I tried to fight the smile but failed miserably.

"I *dig* this," Patrick said, waving his fingers between Nathan and me.

I shook my head at him. "You're the worst." I hissed and then got into the first store I saw.

Patrick and Nathan were grinning when they walked in behind me. I shook my head and tried to get lost in between the clothes.

"I think I was wrong about him."

I smiled at the sound of Nathan's voice behind me. I kept looking at the scarfs, avoiding his stare. I rolled my eyes. "Really?"

I heard him take a step closer to me. I could feel the heat from his body on my back. I felt him reach out and move my hair away, exposing my neck. We were behind a rack so no one could see us...except maybe the cameras in the store, but I didn't really care in that moment.

"I *still* want him to stay away from you," he said softly.

I smiled. "I am not a toy, Nathan."

"*You are mine*," he said in low voice. I could feel his hot breath against my neck; it was easily turning into one of the best sensations in the world. "Mine only," he repeated before leaning in and placing a soft kiss on the crook of my neck.

He was going to be the death of me.

I turned around and faced him. "I'm still not a toy."

"I know you're not," he said with a smile.

"I'm a person," I whispered stupidly. "What is that?" I asked when I saw he was holding something.

He raised his hand and I realized he was holding a small yellow flower. I thought I remember seeing those flowers in one of the bushes we passed earlier. "For you," he said, handing it to me.

I shook my head with a smile as I took it.

"Hannah?" I heard Patrick call somewhere around the store.

Nathan took a few steps back.

"There you are!" Patrick said when he saw me. "What do you think? Hot?" he said, waving a dress.

"Why don't you just get her jewelry or something?"

"You're the one who chose this store," he reminded me.

I shrugged. "I think a necklace is much easier."

He nodded. "Ok, but a *sexy* necklace. You know, one that says 'I want you in bed tonight'," he said, winking at me.

I laughed. "You're wild."

"You bet your ass I am," he said with a smirk.

"Ew. Why do you have to sexualize everything?" I asked as we began to make our way outside.

"Makes my life juicier. You should try it sometime."

~

"Can we eat before we leave? I'm hungry," I said after we finally walked out of the jewelry store.

Turned out that Patrick was the worst person to shop with. He took forever deciding between two different necklaces, it was ridiculous. I wondered if he was always like this with all the girls he dated.

Patrick rolled his eyes at me. "Of course, you are." He looked at Nathan. "I would think twice before dating her, mate, because all your money will go on food, I promise."

Nathan actually chuckled.

"Very funny," I said but I was laughing too. The thought of dating Nathan put me in an unusual good mood. I could see us going to the movies after dinner, holding hands while walking down the street. I shook my head; even I was embarrassed of my own thoughts. Thank God no one could hear them. Without thinking, I turned to look at Nathan who was looking at me. He winked at me as if he knew exactly what I was thinking. I looked away sheepishly.

We decided to go for Chinese food but the restaurant was packed so we had to stand in line. Patrick was telling me something about the last time he saw his parents when Nathan was suddenly on my face.

"We need to go. *Now*," he demanded reaching for my arm.

I looked up at him. "What? Why? What's wrong?"

He placed his hand on the back of my head and pulled me to his chest, as if trying to cover my face.

"Nathan—" I heard myself mumble.

"There is a group of teenagers on one of the tables to your left," he said in my ear. "They were taking pictures of you. We need to leave."

91

He didn't even let me answer and just began to walk out. I looked down at the floor as he kept his grip around me.

I never understood why people would want to take pictures of me. I understood why they followed my brothers, especially Derek who was the most famous of us, but me? I had nothing. I was no one. I was only my dad's daughter. I wasn't interesting. When my dad's fame went to the clouds, they began to follow me around. I guessed they did it to find out more about my dad? Get a good picture of his boring daughter? I didn't understand. Even if they got a good picture, I wasn't a good story.

"Can we stop for a moment?" I asked, pulling myself from his grasp.

I realized we were in the parking lot, I could see the car from where I was.

"Aren't you exaggerating a little?" I asked Nathan, crossing my arms on my chest.

"Hannah, they were taking pictures that will probably be uploaded to social media and then everyone will know where you are and this trip would have been useless."

"He's got a point, Hannah," Patrick said standing next to Nathan.

I shook my head, annoyed. "I *hate* this. I just wanted food."

Nathan chuckled. "We'll get something on the way back."

Patrick began walking back to the car and Nathan took a step towards me. "Could I ask you to do one thing for me?"

"Yes."

"Please, when it comes to your safety, please listen to me." He reached out and put a strand of my hair behind my ear. "I don't know what I would do if anything happened to you," he said softly.

I stared into his mesmerizing green eyes that always seemed to make my brain work slower whenever I looked into them. He didn't know this, but no one had ever told me something like that before. No one had showed so much interest in keeping me safe. Of course, I wasn't going to tell him that so I just whispered, "Okay."

CHAPTER 17

I stared at the white ceiling of the room. Why couldn't I sleep? I was exhausted. All I wanted was to sleep but all my brain wanted to do was think. Think about Nathan and how much I liked being around him.

It was dangerous.

I knew it.

I sighed as I rolled over to the side of the bed, suddenly missing home. I missed my dad and Nick and Rachel—even my mom—who hadn't once called me to ask how I was. Christmas was a week away and I found myself wishing I was in New York.

The door opened and I sat up quickly. I squinted my eyes when Patrick turned on the light.

"Ow," I complained, shutting my eyes.

"You must ask him to come inside," Patrick said as he walked in.

"What?" I asked, still trying to adjust my eyes to the light.

"Ask Nathan to come inside," Patrick repeated. "He's planning on staying outside, you know, to make sure you're safe, but he must be really tired." He gave me a half-smile. "He must really like you."

I rolled my eyes at him. "Or maybe he's just doing his job?"

"We both know it's more than that," Patrick said.

"Where are you going?" I asked trying to change the subject. I noticed that he was wearing jeans with a white button-down shirt. He looked too handsome for someone who's planning to stay at home. I could also smell his cologne from where I was sitting.

"With a friend," he said with a wink. "You and Nathan have the place to yourselves," he said, wiggling his eyebrows at me.

"Shut up," I said, throwing a pillow at him.

He laughed as he made his way out. "Love you too!" he yelled.

"Just go to sleep Hannah," I whispered to myself in my room.

Oh, who was I kidding?

With a defeated sigh, I stood up and made my way downstairs. I was barefoot and was only wearing my pajama shorts with a shirt that I regretted as soon as I opened the main door. It was cold tonight.

"Hannah? Is everything alright?" Nathan asked as soon as he saw me, his eyes were scanning my body.

"No," I told him. "You need to go sleep."

"I don't need sleep."

I crossed my arms on my chest. "Bullshit."

He turned to look at me with an amused look on his face. "Hannah Collins, you have a very dirty mouth."

I shook my head with a smile. "Just come inside and get some sleep, okay?" I asked.

He smirked. "With you?"

I rolled my eyes at him. "Is everything a joke to you?"

"No," he said as he looked away. He was looking outside, which was basically the parking lot and the beach. I could see some shadows of people playing volleyball but other than that, there were no other people close by.

"Nathan, there's no one outside." I reached for his hand. "Come inside."

He smiled. "You know I can't say no to you."

I turned around so he wouldn't see my smile and pulled him inside.

94

"You really do have nice legs, Collins," Nathan said as he shut the door.

"Shut it," I said, feeling self-conscious.

He sat down on the couch and I looked at him for a moment. It was crazy how good-looking he was. He always wore identical suits, yet he still amazed me.

He opened his arms. "Come here."

I didn't even hesitate. I crossed the living room and sat next to him. He put his arm around my shoulders as he turned on the TV and flickered through the channels.

"So you dragged yourself out of bed to get me to come inside and you say you don't like me?" he asked as he settled for a movie.

It was the movie *Elf*, which happened to be one of my favorite movies. I loved to watch this movie during the holidays.

"I never said I don't like you," I said slowly as I watched the movie.

"So you like me?" Nathan asked, glancing at me.

"I didn't say that either," I teased him.

"So you don't feel anything when I touch you?" he said as he ran his fingers over my arm. The goosebumps betrayed me.

"You know I do," I tell him.

"So you like me."

I rolled my eyes at him. "Does your ego need to hear me say it?"

He chuckled. "Actually, yes."

I turned to look at him. "I find you attractive."

He grinned as he stroked my cheek. "Go on."

I shook my head with a smile. "And I like you."

"I like you too, Collins." I smiled as he leaned in to kiss me.

"And I love kissing you," he said against my lips.

His hand went around my waist as he stood up and laid me down on the couch. His lips didn't leave mine one second. When we ran out of breath, he kissed my forehead, down to my cheeks. I felt something inside of me explode when I feel his lips against my neck. I ran my hand through his soft hair as I pulled my head back to give him more access.

His hands went down to the hem of my blouse and I felt him pull it up. We parted for a second so he could pull it over my head. I felt him kiss my collarbone and then pull down the strap of my bra as he put his arms around my waist. I put my legs on either side of his torso as he reached for me, placing me on his lap. His big hands stranded my waist as he kissed me passionately. I pulled his jacket off and then loosened his tie and then began to unbutton his shirt. We were moving so fast like we were running out of time.

I stared at his chest in awe. The outline of his abs was visible and I couldn't help but place my hand against his chest and trace it down to his abs. He was perfect. I had never felt this attraction towards anyone before. It was a foreign feeling. I wanted him.

He placed his hand on my thigh as he pulled me closer to him.

He kissed my lips. "You're driving me crazy," he said breathlessly then he rested his head against my chest.

The only sound was the sound of our heavy breathing as we tried to catch our breath.

"Maybe we shouldn't—" Nathan whispered against my chest.

I felt something in my stomach dropped. This was too good to be true after all.

We didn't move for a long time.

I suddenly felt Nathan press his lips against the center of my chest. "You smell so good," he whispered as he finally looked up and met my gaze. "I want you, Hannah." I bit my lower lip. "You're not helping," he told me looking at my lips.

He looked so helpless.

I was confused. I wanted to ask him what was holding him back but I didn't. Mostly because I knew that sleeping with him would only complicate things. At the same time, I wanted to throw the towel and just do it. I had never liked someone like I liked Nathan. Just being around him made my skin burn. My body was starting to yearn for him. I wanted to be around him all the time.

"I wished I had a good excuse but truth is—" he gave me a crooked smile, "—I don't have a condom on me."

I laughed. "That's okay." I tried to stand up but he placed his hands on my hips, keeping me on his lap.

I knew that if we looked in Patrick's room, we would find one but I also thought about how maybe this was a sign that we shouldn't do it. At least not now.

I looked at him. "Maybe we should just sleep."

He smiled. "I'll like that."

I tried to stand up and again and this time he didn't stop me. I reached for my shirt and threw it over my head. My skin was still tingly from his kisses. I already missed them.

Nathan grabbed his jacket and tie and followed me up to my room. We didn't turn on the light. In the darkness and got under the covers. I lay on my side, and I felt as he pressed himself on my back, wrapping his arm around my waist.

It felt so good to be in his arms. It made me wonder how I had ever been able to sleep without him.

My eyes were closing shut when I felt him kiss the crook of my neck and whisper, "Good night, my Hannah."

CHAPTER 18

Patrick stared at me from across the table with his wide blue eyes. His hair was very messy and he was only wearing jeans with a green sweater but he still managed to pull it off.

"What?" I almost screamed at him as I took a sip of the coffee.

"I didn't take you out to dinner for nothing," he hissed

"I knew you were being too nice," I teased as I used my fork to take a piece of chicken from my plate.

"Hannah," he warned.

I laughed. "What?"

"This isn't funny. I'm your best friend."

"I never said you weren't."

"Best friends tell each other everything."

"They do," I agreed, a smile playing on my lips.

He narrowed his eyes at me. "Then why haven't you explained why I saw Nathan walk out of your room this morning?"

I didn't say anything for a moment. This morning, I actually woke up with a smile on my face. I felt good. I loved sleeping with Nathan. I remembered waking up in the middle of the night with him cuddling me.

Patrick was out all day so Nathan and I spent the afternoon together. We went to watch a movie and then took a long walk on the beach. He had shyly reached for my hand and the thought still made me smile.

I glanced at Nathan through the window glass. It was dark outside but I could still see him as he was parked right outside. He was looking radiant in his suit as he leaned on the car and talked on the phone. Patrick had asked him to give us some privacy, obviously because he wanted me to tell him what happened between Nathan and me last night. That was the thing…

"Nothing happened," I said, trying not to sound disappointed. I was disappointed that nothing had happened between me and Nathan, but I was contented with him just sleeping with me. It had still been a good night.

"Liar," Patrick accused me.

"I am not," I said, looking at him. "We didn't do anything."

He stared at me with his mouth open. "Are you telling me that Hannah didn't get the banana?"

I couldn't help but laugh. "You're unbelievable," I said, laughing.

He chuckled. "I'm sorry. I'm confused, he's gay then?"

"No!" I said quickly then looked down. "He—we—didn't have a condom," I said quietly.

There were families all around us. I didn't want to be the reason the parents had to explain what a condom was to a five-year-old.

Patrick frowned. "What?! I have boxes of condoms in my room!"

I rolled my eyes at him. "I figured."

"So? Why didn't you go get one?"

I shrugged. "I don't know. I figured that maybe it was a sign. Sleeping with him would complicate things."

"So?" he asked again. "If you want to do it with someone, do it. Worry about the consequences later. That's why they're called *consequences*."

"He would lose his job."

Patrick rolled his eyes at me. "You know what your problem is? You think too much. Don't think, just do."

I stared at him in amusement. "I can't believe you just quoted Barney Stinson."

Come to think of it, he was actually *a lot* like Barney Stinson. I watched way too much *How I Met Your Mother*.

99

"I'm being serious," he insisted. "Stop thinking. You want that piece of meat? Eat it."

I laughed. "You know, no wonder you go around sleeping with everyone. You don't even think of them as *people.* " I shook my head at him. "Shame on you."

He shrugged. "At least I don't regret things I *didn't* do."

I frowned at that. He was right. Maybe I did regret not looking for a stupid condom.

I sighed. "Whatever. I don't want to talk about this anymore."

Thankfully, Patrick actually changed the subject. He began to vent about his parents again. He wouldn't admit it, but I knew he was hurt because his parents never spent a lot of time with him. They weren't even coming for Christmas, or asked him to go to New York to celebrate it with them. I felt bad for him.

I knew how it felt to be neglected by a parent, I couldn't even begin to imagine how it felt to be neglected by *both*. In my case, my mom's lack of interest in my life hurt but I knew my dad loved me enough for the both of them. I knew I could always count on him to always be there for me. Patrick didn't.

We finished dinner and then got in line to pay.

"You should still go visit them, Patrick. I'm sure they'd be happy to see you," I said, trying to be optimistic. The line moved and we took a step forward.

"As if," he said. "I'm not going to go to them if they don't want me. They won't probably be home anyway."

I put my hand on his arm. "I'm so sorry. You don't deserve this, Pat."

He shrugged. "Maybe I do. I was never the perfect kid growing up."

"You don't," I assured him. "They're just so busy with their jobs, so consumed by it that they don't realize what they're doing to you."

"Whatever." He looked away and then nudged my arm with a sad smile. "Who needs them anyway, right?"

100

I was smiling at him when Nathan suddenly burst into the restaurant, running and shouting.

"Get on the floor!" he shouted, looking at me and waving his hands up and down.

"What?" I thought I say but I couldn't even hear my own voice. Everyone was staring at him, looking around with confused and scared looks on their faces.

"Get down!" he screamed. Time seemed to slow down as he ran towards me. When he reached me, he wrapped one of his arms around my waist and pressed my head onto chest. I felt as he threw both of us on the floor just as soon as I heard two gunshots.

Everyone instantly panicked when first one fired. I heard loud screams and people running around. I thought I felt someone trip over me. When I heard a woman scream, I knew that the second shot hit someone. I tried to raise my head to look but Nathan held me tightly that it was impossible for me to move.

Patrick. Patrick. Patrick.

Another gunshot came after another, again and again. It was terrifying. I covered my ears to block out the gunshots and the screams and cries from everyone in the room, especially the loud ones coming from the children. That was when I realized what was going on. It hit me like a giant pile of bricks. They found me.

Whoever shot Nick—whoever was trying to hurt my family had found me. I was the next target. And there was nowhere for me to run.

I pressed my face closer to Nathan's strong chest, trying to block what was going on around me. I tried to concentrate on Nathan's heartbeat which didn't help because it was almost beating as fast as mine. I didn't know how much time had passed before I felt him shake me gently. I didn't want to open my eyes.

"Hannah, it's okay. It's over," he whispered in my ear.

I opened my eyes but my vision was blurry anywhere I looked. That's when I realized that it was because I was crying.

Nathan frowned. "Don't cry." I felt him pull me to my feet and put his arms around me. "Don't cry, it's okay,"

I shook my head but I couldn't stop crying. In the distance, I could hear the sound of sirens and there was a lot of noise in the room. A lot of people were screaming, crying, talking, shouting.

"Hannah." I felt Patrick grab my arm and pulled me away from Nathan.

"Oh, God. Thank God you're okay," Patrick said as he embraced me.

I felt relieved. Both Nathan and Patrick were okay. The same couldn't be said about everyone else. As Patrick led me outside, I could see blood on the floor and see sheets over bodies on the ground. I counted three were hit. I prayed that those were the only ones. Broken glasses were all over the floor. I heard them crack as we stepped on them.

Ambulances and police cars were already outside. There were people scattered around, crying. Some were being given first aid, others were talking to police officers.

Patrick stayed with me as Nathan spoke to two cops.

I finally seemed to stop crying but I still felt the knot on my throat. This had all been my fault. I had blood on my hands. Blood of the innocent people who were accidentally killed because of me.

"Ms. Collins," one of the cops said when they reached me and Patrick. "We would like to ask you a few questions."

"I don't know anything," I whispered.

He still proceeded to ask me questions I obviously didn't know the answers to.

I didn't know who was behind the shootout.

I didn't know who was after my family.

I didn't know why they had targeted me.

I didn't know how they found me.

I didn't know anything.

Nathan had a long conversation with them. I waited with Patrick while he talked on the phone with my dad because I was still a bundle of nerves.

After the cop had finally let Nathan go, he approached me. "We are going to the police station. Your father is going to send his private jet and then you and I will be heading back to New York."

I didn't know what else to say so I just nodded and followed him back to the car. Patrick sat with me in the backseat as Nathan drove.

I hated this. All those people got hurt because of me. It was hard not to blame myself.

I stared out the window as I tried to not hate myself for being a Collins.

CHAPTER 19

The next few hours were the longest hours of my life. When we got to the police station, they interrogated all of us individually. I felt useless because I could not answer any of their questions. I wish I knew who was doing this. Didn't they know I would tell them if I did?

After we were finally cleared, Patrick went to the condo to pack our things. Nathan and I waited in an empty room. I sat on the floor and hugged my knees, resting my forehead on my arms. Nathan was pacing around the room, making me feel even more anxious.

After a moment, he finally sat down next to me. "I'm sorry," he whispered.

I turned to look at him. I hadn't realized how tired he looked. His hair was messy and he just looked down—almost angry.

I shook my head. "None of this is your fault, Nathan."

He shut his eyes then leaned his head back. "I feel like I let you down. I should have done something."

"You couldn't have done anything. Please don't blame yourself for this." I reached for his hand and squeezed it. He opened his eyes and looked at me. "You saved my life, Nathan. Thank you." I reached out and kissed his lips.

He smiled but he still looked out of it. I could tell there was something bothering him.

"What's going to happen now?" I asked, resting my head on his shoulder.

"We'll go back to New York. There's no point in staying here now."

I sighed. "I don't understand why someone would do this. To hurt me. To hurt my family. They killed a lot of innocent people…" I trailed off, thinking of the blood I had seen.

Nathan didn't say anything and the room was filled with silence again. This was not how I wanted to go home but I tried to comfort myself. At least I was going home.

When Patrick arrived, we drove to the airport where my father's private jet was waiting.

Patrick kissed my cheek and then hugged me tightly. "I'm so glad you're safe, Hannah. Please stay safe."

I smiled against his shoulder. "You too. I'm sorry we had to leave like this."

He smiled sadly. "Me too. Text me when you land so I know you're safe."

I kissed his cheek. "Okay." I smiled at him before following Nathan into the airplane. I sat by the window and waved at Patrick as we got ready to depart. I hated the fact that I had to leave like this. I was going to miss my best friend.

"How long is it to New York?"

"We'll be there in about three hours."

I nodded. I was beginning to feel a little better. I had washed my face back at the station since I didn't like the feeling of dried tears on my face. The cold water had woken me up a bit. I felt more alert.

The first hour in the plane actually went by fast. I loved looking out the window. Everything looked so small. I especially loved the clouds. They brought me peace.

"Can I ask you something?" Nathan asked after a long moment of silence.

"Yeah?" I asked turning to look at him.

"What's going to happen to us when we land in New York?" he asked.

"I don't know," I admitted.

105

He nodded. "I was afraid you were going to say that."

"Why do you say it like that?"

He smiled. "I've been kicking myself in the ass for not making you mine when I had the chance."

His words made my face grow hot.

Making you mine.

I reached out and placed my hand on his cheek. "Me too," I teased.

He laughed. "Don't tell me that."

I kissed him, hard, knowing that this was probably the one time we were going to be alone in a long time. I missed him already. His kiss was also comforting after the horrible thing we went through today. He made me feel better. He made everything brighter.

When we pulled away, he placed his hands on each of my cheeks and looked at me. "I want you, Hannah," he repeated the same sweet words he had said the previous night. His green eyes seemed darker and I could see desire in them.

I felt that same warm feeling in my stomach I felt whenever I was with him.

Don't think, just do.

In that moment, I chose not to think about anything.

I chose not to think about what had happened in Miami.

I chose not to think about what would happen in New York.

I chose to live the present.

I wanted Nathan.

I needed him now more than ever.

So I took off my seatbelt and sat on his lap. His hands encircled my waist and I put my hands around his neck and pressed myself closer to him.

I didn't care that we were on a plane or that the co-pilot could walk in on us any second. I just cared about Nathan.

He held me as he stood up and laid me on the floor. We were on the seats all the way to the back so I knew we were covered. It was like our little secret spot.

I took his jacket off and then his tie and shirt and ran my hands over his perfect chest. I wasn't holding back anymore.

Nathan pulled my blouse over my head, leaving me in my bra. He kissed my neck; his kisses were urgent and hard. His hands went to the back of my bra and I pulled myself up so he could undo it.

He stared at me when he took it off. I felt myself blush.

"You are so beautiful," he said as he leaned in to kiss me. He went down to my chin, down to my neck, and I heard myself moan when I felt him in between my breasts.

I suddenly felt desperate. I needed him, right now.

"Please tell me you have a condom," I said breathlessly.

He grinned when he looked up at me. "You're not going to catch me unprepared ever again," he said as he reached for his back pocket. He leaned back and I suddenly felt exposed. I watched as he unbuckled his belt then unzipped his pants. I couldn't look away as he pulled them down, revealing a big bulge underneath his boxer briefs.

Not wanting to wait, I pulled my pants down as he put on the condom. I smiled up at him when he finally hovered over me again. He kissed me with urgency as his hands pulled my panties down my hips.

I felt my eyes widened when I felt him go inside of me. He kissed my neck as he began to move. I closed my eyes and leaned my head back.

"*Oh, Nathan,*" I gasped as I gripped his strong arm.

He wasn't as good as I thought he was going to be—he was even better.

CHAPTER 20

We changed quickly and quietly. Nathan headed to the restroom while I sat back down on the seat. I didn't look at Nathan when he came back. My heart was beating so fast, I was sure he could hear it. I could still feel his lips against my body—my insides felt warm and tingly just thinking about it.

A moment later, the co-pilot walked in through the door. I couldn't help but think about what would have happened if he had walked in just a little earlier.

"We are landing in fifteen minutes," he said. "Please put your seatbelts on."

We nodded and simultaneously reached for our seatbelts and strapped them on as the co-pilot headed back through the door. I sat there and stared at the back of the seat in front of me.

I just had sex with my bodyguard.

Here.

On a *plane*.

What the hell were you thinking, Hannah?

Damn Patrick and his *don't think, just do*.

"I can't believe we did it," I whispered, breaking the silence between us.

"Yeah, that was a little wild, even for me." Nathan chuckled.

I shook my head with a smile. "My dad would kill me if he found out what we did on his plane." I looked around. "There aren't any cameras, right?"

"Relax." Nathan placed his hand on top of mine and I finally looked up at him. His green eyes were a lighter green again

108

and I found myself smiling when I saw amusement in his eyes. "That was kind of amazing."

"Yes," I agreed. "It was."

He leaned in and kissed me. "You're mine now, Collins," he whispered against my lips. "*Really* mine."

I smiled as I looked away.

I looked out the window and realized that the plane was ready to land. I closed my eyes as I felt it go down. After a while, the plane finally came to complete stop. I unfastened my seatbelt and stood up. Nathan surprised me by putting his arms around me and planting a kiss on my lips.

"Just in case." He smiled.

The pilot came through the door. "Mr. Collins is waiting for you, miss."

I smiled at him. "Thank you."

I took a deep breath as they opened the door. It was time to go back to the real problems. Images from what had happened in Miami were starting to flood my mind again. A cold breeze hit me; goosebumps rushed through my body but I half smiled.

I was back home.

I saw my dad waiting for us by a black car. I also noticed that more bodyguards were scattered around, looking out.

Nathan suddenly put his arms on my shoulders.

I felt my eyes widen. My dad was watching. "Nathan what—" I stopped when I realized that he was placing my coat. I smiled at him. "Thanks," I said as I slipped my arms through the sleeves.

He just nodded with his poker face. He was in bodyguard mode.

I went down the stairs and half ran to meet my dad. He embraced me in a tight hug. "I'm so glad you're okay," he told me.

I smiled against his chest. "I missed you, Dad."

After a moment, he let me go and smiled at Nathan. "I will be forever grateful to you for taking care of my daughter, Nathan," he said as he shook his hand.

I couldn't look at Nathan but I saw him nod from the corner of my eye.

"Let's go home," my dad said, kissing the top of my head.

I smiled in response. I never thought I would miss home this much but I was happy to be back. We got in the backseat of the car. Nathan went in the passenger seat while another bodyguard drove.

"How's Nick?" I asked as the car started moving.

"He's better. Tired of being in bed. He's like a little boy all over again."

"Dad—" I looked up at him. "I feel horrible about what happened in Miami—all those people—"

"It's not your fault." He sighed. "I understand why you would feel guilty about it, believe me, but the truth is that it wasn't your fault. It's not anyone's fault," he said as he stared at something in a distance. "Your mother has been waiting for you," he said after a moment.

I frowned. "Mom?" She hadn't even called me once.

My dad nodded but he didn't look convinced. "Just—keep an open mind."

"That can't be good," I said.

He shrugged. "How's Patrick?"

I told him some details of my stay in Miami. I told him about Patrick and how beautiful the beach was. By the time we got home, I noticed there were even more bodyguards all around the house. I could see the shadows of them on the roof. They were everywhere.

It was dark, and I suddenly felt exhausted as I got out of the car.

"Hannah," my dad called behind me.

I looked at him. "Huh?"

"Your mother—she's waiting for you and I know you're tired," he said. "Why don't you go through the back door?"

"Why is she waiting?"

110

He sighed. "You don't want to know. At least not right now. Just get some sleep. We'll talk about it tomorrow." He kissed my forehead.

I nodded. I didn't know what my mom was up to but I didn't have the energy to care. I made my way to the back door, the door that was used by employees. The kitchen was empty—it was late so everyone had gone home. I heard laughter coming from the living room and I slipped through a crack that I knew was a blind spot.

I walked straight to the restroom when I reached my room. I took a long, hot shower and it was then when everything began to rush back in. The images what happened in the restaurant in Miami—the blood, the bodies—came back to me and I began to cry.

I felt horrible. Those people died in vain—it was me they wanted dead. I wished we knew who was doing this to me—to my family.

And then I thought about Nathan. Him and what just happened between us. What we just shared on the plane. Something was wrong with me. I couldn't bring myself to regret it—I just couldn't. I loved it. It was magical and amazing, and I knew that I didn't want it to be our last time it.

You're mine now, Collins.

Yes, yes, I was.

CHAPTER 21

The next morning, I woke up to someone shuffling me.

"Stop," I groaned, my voice hoarse from sleeping. My eyes flew open when I felt myself fall off the bed.

"Wake up!"

I frowned at my mom from the floor. "Mom? What's going on?" I asked, pulling my hair away from my face.

"Get dressed!" she said as she pulled the curtains open. "Breakfast is ready and we have guests."

"What?" I asked and stood up. "I don't want breakfast, I want sleep." I got back on the bed.

What was she up to? I couldn't remember the last day she was in my room. *Was this her warm welcome?*

"Hannah Collins," she warned, giving me the look.

"I'm tired," I complained.

She glared at me from the doorway. "You can sleep later. Right now, you have to get downstairs. Don't make me come for you again," she warned before walking out, shutting the door behind her.

I sighed then checked the time.

8:13 am

With another sigh, I got off the bed.

I washed my face and brushed my teeth. My hair wasn't agreeing with me so I put it up on a high ponytail, I didn't want to deal with it right now. I changed into jeans with a pale pink long sleeved blouse and then made my way out of the room slowly. I could hear loud noise coming from the living room when I reached the stairs.

112

I was so not in the mood to socialize. That fact almost made me want to turn around and hide back in my room but my mom hadn't paid so much attention to me in a long time and the person she wanted me to meet must be important to her, I didn't want to disappoint her. Having her attention felt nice. She was acknowledging me again.

With that in mind, I took a deep breath and walked down the stairs. My eyes landed on our dining table. Since our family hadn't been eating together, our table, although not too large, felt huge to me. Today, my mom sat at the table with two other strangers.

Three pairs of eyes looked at me when I walked in.

Geez.

"Good morning?" I greeted awkwardly.

My mom stood up and walked to me quickly. She was wearing a maroon pencil dress with black high heels. Her hair was pulled back but she still looked beautiful. She placed her hand on my back and pushed me forward.

The two strangers stood up and looked at me as we approached them.

"Hannah, this is Lisa. She is an old friend from high school," my mom said with a smile.

I looked at Lisa. She seemed to be my mom's age. She had short blond hair and round hazel eyes. She was wearing black dress pants with a blue button-down blouse. She had a lot of jewelry on her: two earrings on each ear, a necklace, and a lot of rings and gold bracelets in both of her wrists.

She smiled as she offered me her hand. I shook it. "I am so happy to finally meet you. Your mother has told me all about you."

"Really?" I asked, turning around to look at my mom.

My mom ignored my comment and continued on. "This is her son, George."

George was tall with a slim but toned body. He had short blond hair and hazel eyes. He resembled his mom except that he wore square glasses. He was wearing a red button-down shirt that was tucked into his khaki dress pants.

He smiled as he reached for my hand and shook it. "It's nice to meet you, Hannah."

"Thank you," I said, suddenly feeling my face grow hot though I didn't know why.

He kept smiling at me, and Lisa and my mom were staring at us, as if waiting for us to do something. It was so awkward.

"Okay," I finally said and took a seat next to my mom which happened to be in front of George.

"Lisa and George live in Oregon but came here for vacation. They are staying with us for a few weeks," my mom said as they all took their seats.

"Okay," I repeated.

Why were they staying in our house? Couldn't they rent a hotel or something? I mean if Lisa was such a good friend of my mom then why hadn't she mentioned her? Everything was clear now. My mom was trying to set me up with George. What was her problem? This wasn't the first time she tried something like this. Last year, she tried setting me up with some other guy too.

Did she really think she could choose who I dated?

I thought about how I didn't make the best choices when it came to choosing guys but at least it was my choice—they were *my* mistakes.

"Your mother tells us that you like designing," Lisa commented as we ate.

"Oh, I do. I'm still learning though," I said without looking at her.

"But she's really good," my mom said.

I turned to look at her. Who was she trying to fool? She had never once complimented my drawing and now I was suddenly good?

"When are you graduating?" George asked.

"I still need one more year," I answered, trying not to sound as mad as I was. I knew it wasn't his fault—this was all my mom's.

My mom and Lisa started to carry a conversation, probably hoping George and I would do the same but I stuffed my mouth with food, eating as fast as I could. I couldn't even taste what I was eating. After a moment, I stood up with my plate.

"Hannah—" my mom called after me. "What are you doing?"

"I'm done eating," I said with a shrug.

"So leave the plate so they could pick it up!" she hissed, motioning to the maid who was standing by the side. She was looking at me as if I was disrespecting her by picking up my plate.

"Mom, you taught me good manners," I said. "So, I'm picking up my own plate."

Without another word, I turned around and headed to the kitchen. I leaned against the door for a moment, staring up at the ceiling.

What was wrong with my mom?

People had died yesterday—someone was out to kill me or everyone in our family and all she could think about was hooking me up with some rich boy? What was inside her brain that kept her from caring? From worrying about what was happening? About the real issues?

Then again I did have sex with my bodyguard yesterday on a plane so maybe I was just as messed up as she was.

I looked down, and realized that everyone was looking at me.

The bodyguards were having breakfast. I could tell that I had interrupted a conversation because they were all staring at me in silence. Nathan frowned at me, holding his forkful of pancakes mid-air.

I blushed. "Uh—sorry," I murmured then walked to the sink, realizing I was still holding the plate.

115

"I got it, sweetie," Mary, one of the maids said as she took the plate from my hands.

I smiled at her, still feeling everyone staring at my back. "Thanks," I said as I leaned against the fridge. Everyone at the table began to get back to their conversations. The room was loud again. Nathan stood up and walked to me. He crossed his arms on his chest as he stood in front of me. "Is everything okay?" he asked quietly.

"No," I told him. "My mom—" the kitchen door opened and George walked in with the dirty plate in his hands.

He grinned at me. "That was cool."

I frowned as Nathan took a step back. "What are you talking about?"

"What you did back there," he said as he walked closer to me as he set the plate on the sink. "You have some guts," he said as if disobeying your mom was out of this world. *Seriously—who was this guy?*

Nathan took a step forward when George tried to reach for me. "Keep your distance, *mate*," Nathan told him, glaring.

George frowned. "I'm sorry—who is he?" he asked me.

I cleared my throat. "He's my bodyguard."

"Oh," George looked at him. "Well, I'm not going to hurt her."

"Keep your distance and *no one* will get hurt," Nathan said, it sounded like a threat.

George looked at me as he shook his head. "Your mom is calling you. Shall we go?"

"You go—I'm right behind you," I said after a moment.

He nodded. "Okay."

"*Be nice*," I hissed at Nathan who placed his hand on the fridge next to me.

He lowered his head, and I looked around nervously. Either everyone was pretending to not notice us or they really were minding their own business because no one was looking at us. Mary was washing the dishes but she had her back to us. Either way, I knew she wouldn't say anything to my mom.

"I don't like it when people touch what's mine," he said in a low voice, looking directly into my eyes which was a bit intimidating. I found myself liking how possessive he was over me though. Was that bad? I liked to feel wanted.

I raised an eyebrow with a smile. "Uh, excuse me?"

"I'm being serious, Hannah," he said.

"You said the same thing about Patrick and you ended up becoming buddies," I reminded him.

"You're mine," he whispered, ignoring my comment.

I smiled. "Okay."

"Okay," he said.

"Okay," I repeated before walking back to the dining room with an amused smile on my face.

CHAPTER 22

"So how was Miami?"

I looked up at Rachel and half smiled. "It was fun..." I trailed off. I didn't really want to talk about Miami. I didn't want to even *think* about Miami. Rachel was in her walk-in closet while Nick sat on the bed. He looked pretty good but he looked bored to death. He was flickering through the channels murmuring something about how there was nothing good to watch.

Rachel sighed as she glanced at him. "He wants to get back to work already," she whispered as she hung a dress. "The doctor said he had to be in bed rest for at least two months. And I don't really want him to go back—not until we find who did this to him."

"I can hear you," Nick said from the bed.

Rachel rolled her eyes then walked out of the closet. I watched as she took out a black binder from her purse and handed it to Nick. "You can work from here."

Nick took it, a smile forming on his lips as he opened the binder. "Why haven't you given it to me?"

"Because I didn't want to see that stupid smile on your face."

Nick chuckled. "You're the best wife ever," he said reaching out and kissing her.

I smiled at them. They really were great together. There was suddenly a knock on the door though it opened and my mom walked in.

"There you are," she said looking at me. "I've been looking all over for you."

I frowned. "Why?"

She handed me a shopping bag. "This is for you to wear tonight."

"Where are we going?"

"I want to show Lisa Colton's club."

"Mom—"

"Don't fight me on this, Hannah. We're going," she interrupted me. She looked at Nick and her expression softened. "How are you doing?"

He waved the binder in his hand. "Great."

My mom smiled. "Good." Then she looked at me again. "Be ready by eight." And then she walked out.

I looked at Rachel and Nick. "Did you guys know what she was planning to do?" Their silence was the answer. I shook my head. "I can't believe she's trying to set me up with George."

"I thought he was cute," Rachel said.

"Rachel, I am twenty-one years old. I am capable of choosing who I want to date," I said as I took out what was in the shopping bag. It was a beautiful strapless red dress. "And my own clothes."

"She just wants what's best for you," Nick said as he looked through some papers.

I shook my head. "This isn't the way to do it."

Rachel walked to me. "So tell her."

I bit my lip. "Is it sad that I'm only doing this because of attention?"

Rachel sighed as she touched my hair. "I'm sure your mother loves you, Hannah. She's your mom."

I looked down. "If she does, she has a funny way of showing it."

"I can be your substitute mom," she offered.

I laughed. "Can I tell you something?"

"Of course, you can, I'm your mom," she said, making me laugh.

I glanced at Nick who was too busy looking through whatever those papers were, and then leaned in to Rachel's ear. "I kind of slept with Nathan."

Rachel looked at me with wide eyes. "Seriously?"

I bit my lip. "I did."

She closed her mouth. "How was it?" she whispered.

I smiled. "It was great."

"So—what does that make you? His girlfriend?"

"I don't know," I admitted. "I honestly like how things are now. It's fun," I said, biting my lip.

"Hannah—you're *glowing*!"

"Shh!" I said.

"What are you two talking about?" Nick asked glancing at us.

"Nothing," I told him looking at Rachel. "You can't tell anyone," I whispered.

"My lips are sealed," she promised then smiled. "I like him for you. He's really handsome and he's such a good guy."

"I know," I sighed as I stood up. "I have to go get ready now. Pray for me."

Rachel smiled. "I'm sure it won't be that bad."

I just shook my head as I made my way out the door. I had showered earlier in the day so I decided to iron my hair straight. The dress wasn't as short as it looked—it went down just above my knees. It was tight around my body but I put on my coat and it didn't look as bad. I wasn't about to put on high heels so I put on black Vans. Maybe I looked ridiculous but I didn't care. The worse I looked, the better.

"What are you wearing?" my mom asked me when she saw me walk down the stairs.

Christmas was the day after tomorrow so the tree was in the living room. I really loved Christmas trees; I loved how the lights looked. It also reminded me that I hadn't done my Christmas shopping.

I looked down. "The dress?"

"With sneakers?"

I had worn it to make her happy and she still found a way to disagree with me.

I sighed. "Mom, it's cold outside. Besides, I don't think anyone is going to notice."

She just shook her head. "Come on, they're waiting outside."

I followed her, sulking. At the same time, I hoped Colton was at the club tonight. I wanted to see him. My mood changed instantly when I saw Nathan opening the door for my mom.

He glanced at me and I looked down with a smile.

"Thank you," I said as I got in the truck. I realized too late that my mom had gone in first because she wanted to sit in the back, with Lisa. Leaving me no option but to sit next to George.

Nathan shut the door and then got in the passenger seat as Robin began to drive.

"You look wonderful," George told me.

I half smiled. "Thanks." I looked out the window, hoping he would get the message that I didn't want to talk. I noticed another duplicate Escalade followed us, probably more bodyguards. My mom was putting us in danger and she either didn't realize it or didn't care. I didn't know which one was worse.

Colton's club was located in New York City. It was like a small club city because it was next to other clubs so it was always flooded with people. Despite the competition, Colton's club which was called Ecstasy, was the most famous. People came from all over. From the outside, it was black with the word Ecstasy glowing in blue. There were two big bodyguards at the entrance who were checking ID's. There was a long line outside, I couldn't even see the end of it. Robin stopped the truck right at the entrance and I opened the door, beating Nathan to it. I stood by him as my mom, Lisa, and George walked out.

It was loud. People were laughing and screaming over the music that already sounded loud and we were still outside.

My mom and Lisa walked ahead, and George looked at me.

"Should we go?" he asked me.

Nathan took a step forward, standing right next to me.

"I'm actually going to look for my brother," I said. "I'll catch up later?"

He shook his head with a smile. "Don't worry. I get it," he said when turned around and followed my mom and Lisa.

I looked at Nathan and raised my eyebrows. "Happy?"

He grinned. "*Very.*"

I shook my head, smiling. "Come on."

The bodyguards let Nathan and me inside. I noticed a few bodyguards had gone after my mom.

Inside, it was dark and loud. *Very* loud.

It was one of the reasons I didn't like clubs, I hated how loud the music was. I reached for Nathan's hand and pulled him with me as I walked along the sidelines. There were people everywhere. Some were at the tables. They were round and small and only held up by a pole. They were high, it wasn't meant for people to sit around, but stand. Others were at the bar around the bartenders who were making drinks faster than my eyes could follow. Most of the people were at the dance floor, dancing and grinding against each other. Colton's office was actually high, on a special second floor just for him. Most people didn't know where his office was, of course. Mostly because it was too dark for them to notice the stairs that were on the back, always guarded by Colton's big bodyguards.

Thankfully, one of them recognized me and nodded at me.

"Is my brother in his office?" I yelled at him over the music.

He nodded then moved to the side, allowing me to walk in.

"He's with me," I told him when he turned to look at Nathan.

We walked up the stairs in silence.

The stairs led straight to Colton's office and we stopped outside the door.

"You should wait here," I told Nathan.

122

He nodded. "Okay."

I looked at him suspiciously. "You're not fighting me on this?"

He shrugged, looking amused. "He's your brother."

"You're a jerk," I teased.

He smiled then put his arm around my waist and he pulled me closer to him. "You look really sexy in that dress," he said, looking down.

I still had the coat on but it was open so you could still see the dress underneath.

I smiled sheepishly. "Thank you."

He met my gaze and then leaned in to kiss me.

It was then, as we kissed, that the door opened next to us.

CHAPTER 23

Nathan and I pulled apart but it was too late. I looked at my brother, Colton, who was wearing a black suit with a black button-down shirt underneath. His black hair was pulled back and he was glaring at Nathan with his blue eyes.

"Hannah—*what?*" he asked, confusion and anger clear in his face.

I took a step in front of Nathan at the same time he did, getting in between them. I placed my hands on Colton's chest. "Colton—*don't,*" I said, trying to push him away but he was strong. "Colton," I repeated when he ignored me. "Stop."

His gaze lowered to me.

"Please...let's go inside," I tried to sound brave but it sounded like a plea. Colton and Nathan were two big men. I wouldn't be able to stop them if they started to fight. At least not without help and then I would have to explain to everyone why Nathan was fighting my brother. Colton had always been the most protective out of my brothers and I knew Nathan wouldn't hold back if Colton started something.

In a way, they were very much alike.

When I tried to push Colton, he actually turned around and walked back into his office. I bit my lip as I closed the door behind us.

"It's not what it seems," I began slowly.

Colton chuckled humorlessly. "Oh, really? Because it seems to me that you are screwing your bodyguard."

I frowned. "Okay...maybe it is what it seems."

Was it that obvious? It was just a kiss, I could have denied it. At the same time, I knew I couldn't fool Colton.

"Hannah, what the hell are you doing?"

I gulped as I watched him from across the room. "I like him."

"Do Mom and Dad know?" he asked.

"No—"

He shook his head. "Well, I can tell you they're not going to be any happier than me."

"I'm an adult," I said, suddenly feeling angry at him. "I can see whoever I want."

"He's your bodyguard."

I nodded. "Exactly. Thanks to him I'm alive. Aren't you the tiniest grateful to him for that?"

He sighed and I watched as his tense shoulders relaxed a little. His eyes softened when he looked at me. "Of course, I am." He shook his head; a smile was playing on his lips. "Come here," he said opening his arms.

I smiled in relief and walked to his arms.

"I still don't like him," he said when he let me go.

"When have you ever liked a guy I've dated?"

He narrowed his eyes at me. "How serious is it?"

I bit my lip. "I don't know. We're just barely figuring everything out. Please don't tell Mom and Dad."

He shook his head but he was smiling. "You let him know he will have to deal with me if he makes you cry."

I frowned, mostly because he had reminded me that all guys seemed to do was make me cry. "Please no threats."

He walked to the small bar he had in his office and poured some wine in a glass.

"Can I have some of that?"

"No," he said.

"I'm twenty-one," I reminded him.

"I don't care."

"I'll just get it downstairs then."

He rolled his eyes at me and handed me his glass then poured himself another one. Colton's office was actually pretty big. He had a desk with papers and his laptop was opened, there was a long, black couch, the small bar with all kind of alcohol and a bathroom. The highlight of his office was the big glass window that faced the club. He could see everything from here. I looked out the window. It was pretty dark but I could make out the people dancing and see the bartenders move quickly as they made drinks. It was ideal for Colton—he liked having control.

I took a sip of the wine. "So, how are you?"

He shrugged as he sat next to me on the couch. "Busy."

"Still whoring around?"

He looked at me and raised his eyebrows. "You stay out of my love life and I'll stay out of yours."

I smiled. "Deal."

"Who are you here with?"

"Mom. Didn't she tell you we were coming? She's trying to set me up with some guy," I rolled my eyes. "I've been running away from him all day."

"As much as I don't like idea of you screwing your bodyguard—you are allowed to be who you want to be with," he said with a frown.

"Thank you!"

"So, tell her."

I shook my head. "No, not yet."

He shrugged. "Then don't complain."

I narrowed my eyes at him. "Okay, *smart-ass*."

He chuckled. "It's good to see you, Hannah."

I smiled at him. "You too. I miss you."

His phone began to ring and he answered it. "Okay," he said after a moment and then hung up. "Mom's on her way up."

I stood up. "That's my cue to leave."

"Please take care," he said as he hugged me again.

I nodded. "You too. I'll see if I can come more often."

"Okay."

He kissed my cheek and then I turned around and walked out before my mom could see me.

Without a word I grabbed Nathan's hand and pulled him down the stairs and out of the club.

"What happened?" he asked once we were outside.

"He's not going to say anything," I said with a shrug. "Let's get out of here."

I waited for Nathan go get one of the trucks and then hoped in when he pulled up.

"You know, just so you know, I would have taken responsibility," Nathan said as he drove.

I frowned. "What are you talking about?"

"If your parents or anyone else found out about us, I would take full responsibility for my actions. I just want you to know that."

I looked out the window as I smiled. "Okay."

"So where am I headed?" he asked after a moment.

"Can we get some food? And then, I don't know." I looked at him. "Take me to your place."

He grinned. "Your wish, my command Collins."

I smiled but didn't say anything. I really wanted to be with him. It was scary how much I missed him. I was starting to get used to being around him.

I wanted to be with him—all the time.

I turned to look at him as he drove. He really was the most handsome guy I had ever been with. He was different.

He had to be different from everyone else.

He *had* to.

CHAPTER 24

We went to get some cheeseburgers. As Nathan drove, it reminded me of our road trip and I thought about how so many things had changed since then.

I was surprised to see that Nathan's apartment wasn't that far from my house. It was about two blocks away.

"It's been a long time since I've been here," he said as he opened the door for me. "I usually spend the night at your house."

I nodded. I knew bodyguards had rooms where they could sleep. I didn't know why it never occurred to me that Nathan stayed there all the time. I ate fries as I followed him up the stairs. The apartments were a creamy color. There were three floors, and Nathan's was on the second. He took out his key and opened it.

Inside, it is warm and it also seemed empty. Not because of lack of furniture, there were brown couches in the living room, a TV, a small dining room table and a few decorations here and there but not much. I could tell he hadn't been there in a long time. It smelled musty and Nathan slid the glass door that led to the balcony, allowing fresh air to vent in.

"This is my humble place," Nathan said.

I walked to the couch and sat down. "It's not bad."

He chuckled softly. "I know it's nothing compared to your mansion—"

"Nathan—" I cut him off. "It's fine," I said with a smile. "When was the last time you were here?"

He shrugged as he took off his jacket. "Before we left for Miami."

I turned on the TV as I took out my cheeseburger.

It was one good looking cheeseburger.

Nathan sat next to me on the couch and threw an arm around my shoulders.

"Did your brother give you a hard time?" he asked as I ate.

"Colton has always been overprotective," I looked at him. "You guys are actually very much alike."

"He looked ready to punch me."

"I know. I was afraid of that," I said then took another bite of the cheeseburger.

"Your mom is trying to set you up with George, isn't she?" he asked after a moment of silence.

"Yes, can you believe it? I'm an adult. She can't just go around and set me up with some stranger."

"You don't like him, right?"

I looked up at him and waited until I swallowed the food to answer him. "Of course not. I like you."

He smiled. "I feel very protective over you."

"Really? I hadn't noticed," I said sarcastically.

"I just—*want you all to myself.*"

I half smiled. "Isn't it enough knowing I don't want anyone but you?"

He offered me a crooked smile. "I like hearing you say it but no." He kissed the side of my head as I put the trash in the bag and set it aside.

"Is there a specific reason or have you always been like this with the girls you've been with?" I asked him as I took a sip of the lemonade. And then I put a piece of gum in my mouth, afraid my breath smelled like onions.

He shrugged. "I just feel like if I don't take care of you, someone is going to snatch you from me under my nose." He leaned in. "You're mine."

I smiled at him. "I'm *yours.*"

He kissed my lips. "I miss you," he said. "I hate seeing you so close to me and not being able to touch you." He kissed me.

129

"I need to go pee," I said against his lips making him laugh but he let me go. "I'll be back," I said. "Uh, where?"

"That door," he said, pointing to the first door down the hall.

"Okay," I said then went in.

After using the toilet, I washed my face. I looked at my reflection in the mirror and saw that my face was flushed. I threw away the gum, satisfied with my minty breath and then headed out. I took off my coat and smiled when I saw Nathan watching me.

"You look sexy in red," he told me as I went back to the couch.

I meant to sit next to him, where I was but he grabbed me by the waist and pulled me so I ended up sitting on his lap. He had taken off his tie and the first few buttons of his shirt were unbuttoned, teasing me.

I rested my head on the crook of his neck as he put his arms around me. We stayed like that for a moment. I felt like a baby and felt so protected in his arms. I pressed my lips on his neck and kissed him, feeling him tense under me. I straightened up as I began to kiss his neck while unbuttoning his shirt.

"*Hannah,*" he whispered as he closed his eyes.

His skin was so soft, and he smelled so good. I couldn't stop kissing him.

I felt him stand up, with me in his arms and began walking to his bedroom. He sat me on the bed gently and I glanced up at him. He took off his shirt. I kicked off my shoes before he hovered over me. My back hit the bed as he leaned in to kiss me on the lips. I felt his hands pulled my dress down, exposing my bra. He unhooked it and threw it out of the way.

I moaned when I felt his hands on my breast. My eyes shut closed.

Nathan was *beyond good.*

I felt so loved in his arms.

So *wanted.*

I never wanted to leave him. I wanted this moment to be frozen forever. I could die right now and I would die happy in his arms.

"You're so beautiful," he whispered as he moved on top of me. "So *beautiful.*"

I couldn't speak. I wanted to tell him that he was the best thing that had ever happened to me; that I didn't care if things didn't work between us; I didn't care if I was in for another heartbreak; I didn't care about anything.

I knew I would never forget him.

I would never forget this night.

I would never forget a minute spent with him.

He could break my heart and I wouldn't care because being *his* was the only thing I cared about.

I knew being his was something I would never forget.

CHAPTER 25

I stared at my house through the window and frowned. "I really don't want to go in there."

It was around five in the morning and we were just coming back from Nathan's place. We had only slept a few hours and I was exhausted but I was also happy. I felt like I could fly and touch the sky. Yes, I was singing that in my head. I didn't know what was going to happen between us. All I knew was that I had never in my life been this happy. I couldn't seem to stop smiling. I was already wondering when I could be with him again.

Nathan shook his head from the driver's seat. "Me either."

His hair was still wet from our shower together; it looked darker and was combed back. He walked out of the truck and went around to open the door for me. He was wearing jeans with a sweater since he left his suits at my house.

He was a dream come true.

"I could kiss you," he said as he opened the door.

I laughed. "That wouldn't be a good idea but I would probably let you."

I nervously looked at all the bodyguards around us. It was starting to get harder and harder for me to hide whatever was happening between Nathan and me.

My body just responded to him.

Across the street, I could see a few cars that I was sure were paparazzi. I hadn't seen them for a while. I thought they had decided to leave us alone. I knew it was their job or whatever but that didn't make them any less annoying. They had been trying to get statements from my family about the incident in Miami. My

132

father had already made a statement and helped the families of the victims. I knew money wouldn't replace their loved ones but I was glad my father was doing something for them.

"I should go inside," I said with a frown.

Nathan nodded and didn't say anything.

I made my way to the house, grateful that no one saw me. Only the maids were up at this hour but they were nowhere in sight. I made my way to my room and slept for a few more hours.

Today was Christmas Eve and it was chaotic the entire day. My mom had me help her and Lisa and—you guessed right— George wrap a few presents. I think she just wanted an excuse to keep me in the room with George. I did my best to look disinterested. It was starting to be really annoying.

Even if I did like George, did they seriously think that we were going to talk instantly connect?

By dinner time, I found myself in a bad mood. I hated admitting it but I knew it was due to the fact that I hadn't seen Nathan since morning.

Was it crazy that I missed him terribly?

Dinner seemed to take forever. My mom then made all of us sit in the living room and have a stupid chat. I didn't even know what they were talking about. I was becoming more pissed at her by the second.

Rachel came and sat next to me on the couch. "Are you okay?" she whispered.

"No," I said. "I hate this."

"She's really going strong about this, huh?" Rachel said glancing at my mom.

"I don't know what makes her think she can just boss me around."

"So why are you letting her?"

It was a good question. I was an adult. I could leave if I wanted to. My dad wasn't even here. He was in his office with Nick.

133

"I don't know," I admitted. "I guess I just really wanted her attention."

"Well, you sure have his attention now," Rachel said, raising her eyebrows.

I followed her gaze and realized that Nathan was standing on the back of the room. He was back in his suit and nodded at me with a smile when he saw me. Just looking at him made me feel better. I looked back at Rachel, suddenly smiling. "He's really something."

Rachel smiled at me. "Why don't you two just make it official?"

I shrugged. "We haven't really talked about it. There's something about seeing him secretly that I really like."

Rachel laughed. "Well, you two should talk about it. It is obvious he likes you and, sooner or later, it will come out."

"Hannah," my mom suddenly called me. I looked up at her. She was by the Christmas tree, taking some pictures. "Come."

With a sigh, I stood up and walked to her.

"Stand next to George, I want to take a picture," she said.

"Mom." I wanted to complain but she was already pulling my arm. George put an arm around my waist. I looked up at Nathan. He was glaring at him. I watched as he turned around and disappeared to the kitchen.

"You look so good together!" Lisa said. I saw Rachel roll her eyes, making me laugh.

"Smile, Hannah," my mom ordered as she raised the camera.

I tried to smile but I knew I hadn't succeeded when I saw my mom frown at the pictures.

"Hannah, where are you going?" my mom asked when I made my way to the front door.

"Outside!" I said, walking out before she could stop me.

I walked to a little bench we had off to the side, surrounded by trees. I hadn't realized George had followed me until he sat next to me.

"You seem annoyed," he commented after a moment of silence.

It was dark and cold outside. I had walked out without my coat and was starting to regret it. It didn't even feel like it was Christmas Eve. Last year, all my family had gathered around the dinner table at around this time. Rachel had made dinner since my dad let the service people take the day off. I had helped Rachel cook and serve. Derek and Colton were there as well. I remembered jokes and laughter, even my mom had been enjoying herself. It had been so intimate and so perfect...nothing like this year.

"I don't have anything against you," I said, looking down at my feet. "I just see what my mom is doing and it's annoying."

He nodded. "Yes, I can tell," he pauses. "So, who is it?"

"What?" I asked looking at him.

"It's obvious you have a boyfriend or at least someone that you like. I've been trying to figure out why you haven't told your mom about *him*."

I thought about denying it but then I thought there was no point. I didn't even care if my mom would find out. I had put up with her little game long enough and I knew it was going to be for nothing because in the end, she was still going to be angry when I told her about Nathan.

"She doesn't even know."

He sighed as he rested his back on the bench. "Well, my mom knows about mine and she doesn't like *her* because her family isn't rich."

"You have a girlfriend?" I asked, looking at him.

He nodded with a smile. "I do and I love her."

"So why are you here?"

He shrugged. "Maybe for the same reason you are—just trying to make my mom happy."

I shook my head. "This is ridiculous. I'm tired of it."

He nodded. "At least I got to meet the famous Richard Collins." He grinned. "I loved his movies."

I smiled. "My dad *is* kind of awesome."

"He is," George agreed then he turned to look at me. "It's the bodyguard, isn't it?"

I opened my mouth to say something but a hand suddenly clasped it closed. George's eyes widened but before he could do something, two men in black jumped from behind and grabbed him.

"Hey!" I heard him scream as he resisted.

Whoever was clasping my mouth closed, grabbed me and pulled me to my feet. I tried to scream but I couldn't.

"Hannah!" I heard Nathan scream from somewhere behind me and then whoever was holding me let me go and when I turned around, I realized Nathan had pulled him away. They were already fighting as I turned around. It was hard to know what was going on because it was dark. Everyone just looked like shadows. I thought I saw George on the ground.

My heart was beating fast. I didn't know what to do.

And then I saw two dark figures walk towards me. I began to take a few steps back but before I could run off, I felt a pang of pain on the back of my head and then my eyes closed as I felt myself fall to the ground.

CHAPTER 26

When I was ten years old, I almost drowned. I was in the pool with my dad and he was swimming with Nick and Colton while I just sat on the stairs and watched them. I remember that I wanted to go to them and began to take steps forward. I couldn't remember how I just lost my grip and then I started to drown. I began to move my arms desperately, making the water splash all over me as I tried to gasp for air.

The feeling of the water pulling me down was one of the worst things I'd ever experienced. It just felt horrible. The water traps you and you can't breathe—no matter how hard you try to gasp for air—and even when you do, the air isn't enough. It's suffocating and you can't breathe and you know you're dying but you can't do anything about it.

This was exactly how I feel when I began to come to my senses—*out of breath*. As if I were drowning or as if I had been running for a really long time.

I tried to gasp but couldn't because I realized that my mouth was taped. I opened my eyes but everything was a blur. I desperately tried to breathe and gasp for air but I couldn't. I tried to move my hands but they were tied behind my back—I tried to stand up but my legs were tied around the chair I was seated on. I heard screams around me as I began to feel suffocated. And then someone ripped the tape off my mouth and I was finally able to breathe properly. I coughed over and over but I couldn't seem to catch my breath. And then, slowly, it began to come back. My heart slowed down and my breathing began to regulate.

"What the hell did I tell you?" I heard a voice scream somewhere around me. "I gave you one order! ONE ORDER! What was it?!"

"To not hurt her, sir," a smaller voice answered.

"Exactly! And what did you do? Look at her!"

I frowned.

Were they talking about me? What was wrong with me? Where was I? Was this a dream? I was on the bench with George and then—and then, oh my god.

I opened my eyes again and blinked until my vision cleared up. It took my eyes a moment to adjust to the brightness in the room. When they did, I looked around. I was in what seemed to be a garage. There were three cars with the hoods up as if someone were in the middle of repairing them. There were mechanic tools all over the floor along with dirty towels. The walls were white but they were dirty, stained with black grease. There didn't seem to be windows and I didn't see any doors. In front of me were two men I had never seen before in my life. One of them was taller with broad shoulders. He was wearing blue jeans with a white T-shirt. He had dirty blond hair and brown eyes. The other one was shorter and chunkier. He was wearing a navy blue mechanic uniform with the name John written on it with white letters.

I opened my mouth to scream but nothing came out. They kidnapped me. They kidnapped me and now I was gonna die. The two men were arguing so they hadn't noticed that I was looking at them.

I tried to turn my head and my heart skipped a beat because right there next to me was Nathan, tied to a chair, his mouth taped. His eyes were closed and he was beaten up with blood coming down from his eyebrow and lip. His white t-shirt was also stained with blood and I realized that he was shot somewhere on the stomach. There was a puddle of blood on the floor.

Oh my god.

Was he dead?

138

"Nathan!" I screamed at him without thinking. "Nathan, please open your eyes!"

But Nathan didn't move. Instead, someone grabbed my chair and turned me around so Nathan was behind me and I couldn't see him anymore. I was crying. I couldn't stop crying because I feared the worst. Nathan was dead.

"Hey," the taller man said as he kneeled in front of me. "Hey, don't cry, baby girl."

"Who are you?" I demanded, trying to sound brave but my voice was shaking and I wasn't sure I was even making sense. "What did you do to him?" I cried.

"Stop crying," he ordered and reached out to wipe the tears on my cheeks. I turned my head to the side, feeling disgusted just by thinking about his touch.

He smirked. "You're even more beautiful in person, Ms. Hannah."

I gulped as I tried to force myself to stop crying. "What do you want? Why are you doing this?"

He stood up in front of me. "It's nothing personal, darling, this is about money. If you behave—nothing's going to happen to you."

I looked at him for a moment, trying to decide whether I should believe him. That was when I saw the wall behind him. It had pictures of me all over it. Pictures from magazines. Most of them I was walking in the street or having dinner with my dad. Others were family pictures with their heads were cut off except for mine. Some of the images where taken when I was in Miami.

He had been following me.

He had been following me. All this time and I never suspected anything. I didn't think it was real—the thought of someone wanting to do anything bad to me and now he had kidnapped me and had probably killed Nathan. My mind was going crazy as I tried to fit all the puzzle pieces together.

"You tried to kill me," I accused the man, looking at him. "In Miami—you tried to kill me and…and you killed those innocent people!"

"We weren't trying to kill you!" the man said. "We were trying to kill him so it would be easier to abduct you!" He pointed to Nathan who was on the floor. "He was never part of the plan but he was always in the fucking way! Always there with you, watching everything. So we had to take him out first. Unfortunately, the son of a bitch caught on to us," he said, nodding his head as he crossed his arms on his chest. "I gotta give it to him—he was quick. Not that it matters because he's going to die anyway.""

"No," I said quickly. "Please don't hurt him. None of this is his fault."

"All of this is his fault. If he weren't so good at his fucking job, we would have gotten to you much sooner." He chuckled as if there were an inside joke. "Now, he's just an itch I have to scratch."

"No," I shook my head. "Please, I'm begging you. Don't hurt him. My dad—he would pay whatever you ask him to pay but please don't hurt Nathan." "Interesting," he said thoughtfully. "You really believe your father would pay to save this fucker's life?"

"Yes," I said quickly. "He would. Just let me speak with him. I'll tell him."

He chuckled. "You think I'm that stupid right? You'd lead him right to us." He turned to look at the other man and shook his head. "This girl thinks I'm an idiot."

The other man chuckled.

"I don't think you're stupid." I sobbed, miserably. "I'm just trying to get you what you want. If you would just let me speak with my dad—"

"Shut up!" he screamed at me then leaned in until his face was only a few inches away from mine. "Shut the fuck up!"

I pursed my lips, forcing myself to stop crying though the tears continued to roll down my cheeks.

"I already told you, I'm not going to hurt you," he said in a quieter voice. "I couldn't hurt you."

I couldn't hurt you? What did he even mean by that? He could definitely hurt me if he wanted to. There were two of them and there was only me now. They were much bigger and stronger. Since when did kidnappers have sympathy for their victims?

He cleared his throat as he straightened up. He looked at me for a moment and I wished I could read his mind. He finally turned around. "Come on, John, let's do some business," he told the other called John.

"Yes, sir," John said as he followed him. They disappeared through a door.

I finally let go and began to sob again. I was so scared. So desperate. *How many days had passed since they took us?* I realized that I was still wearing the dress from Christmas Eve but my shoes were missing. *What happened to George? How did those men able to reach the house without being noticed? Who was that man? But most importantly, what had they done to Nathan?* I just wanted Nathan to wake up. I wanted him to be alive.

I knew they had hit me on the head; there was a constant shot of pain that was there to remind me of it.

The room was quiet for a long time except for my sob and the sound of something. When I was able to clear my sight, I looked around for something—anything that could help me. I spotted a screwdriver on the floor but that was it and it was too far for me to reach. I didn't know what to do, however, *Nathan would.*

"Nathan!" I whispered, looking up at the ceiling. "Nathan, please open your eyes. Please."

He can't die. He just can't.

CHAPTER 27

I didn't know how many times I had heard people say that time didn't exist. I never really thought about it but being tied to a chair with nothing to do but think—well you think about a lot of things. I wanted to know how long I had been there for. Hours? Days? I wanted to know what time it was.

I wanted to run out of here and look up at the sky. Funny how I woke up every day and took all of those things for granted. I didn't know how lucky I was to be alive and free.

How long was this man going to keep me here for? Had he contacted my dad already? How much money was he asking for? Did this man have as much honor as he claimed to have? Or was he going to take the money and kill me after? What was he planning behind that door? Who was he? Those were the burning questions I had been trying to figure out what. And then another thought occurred to me: why did he let me see his face? Maybe he wasn't going to let me go.

I was sweaty and tired and the rope around my hands had gotten tighter and everything hurt. I just wanted to get out of here.

Why won't Nathan wake up?

The sound of the door opening behind me made me want to begin to cry with fear. *What was he going to do with me?*

Don't cry, Collins something Nathan would say. I bit my lip and tried to gulp the knot that was stuck in my throat. I had to be strong if I wanted to save Nathan. He couldn't be dead. He was strong and it was my turn to save him.

The man walked in and took a seat in front of me. He was wearing another pair of jeans with a button-down shirt and black shoes this time. He grinned at me. "I brought you food."

"I'm not hungry," I said, looking away.

"Oh, you're eating," he said as he took a white styrofoam plate out of a plastic bag. "Unless you want me to hurt him?"

I turned to look at him and realized he was talking about Nathan.

He chuckled. "I'm not an idiot, Hannah. I know he is more than a bodyguard to you. I've been watching you two for a while now," he said as he opened the plate. It was Chinese take-out. I could tell because the smell filled the room. "Your parents don't know, do they? They have no idea you're fucking the bodyguard." He chuckled then pointed at me with the fork in his hand. "Oh, you're a naughty girl." He forked some food and brought it to my mouth.

I hated being fed but I opened my mouth. I wouldn't do anything that could hurt Nathan. He was already hurt. I knew I had to do something. I chewed on the food which was tasteless in my mouth.

"Who are you?" I asked him. "Why are you doing this to my family? What did we ever do to you?"

"I told you this is nothing personal," he said. "I want money, Hannah, and your father happens to have millions," he said as he continued feeding me.

He looked at me for a moment then shook his head with a smile. "There are so many things you don't know about your precious family, Hannah."

I looked at him but didn't say anything. For all I knew, he was just trying to mess with my head. My mind was already going crazy. I didn't need any more crazy stories. I shook my head when he tried to feed me another forkful of food. "No more, please," I whispered. I was starting to feel sick. Maybe throwing up on him wouldn't be the worst thing in the world though.

"You're not the only one with dirty secrets," he continued as he placed the plate on the table. He stood up and walked behind me. I heard some movements but didn't know what he was doing until he threw Nathan on the floor, right by my feet. His head was turned the other way. I couldn't see his face but I could see bruises on his cheek. I began to shake as I looked down at his body.

"Please don't hurt him," I begged, scared of what he was going to do.

The man grinned as he looked down at Nathan. "We weren't even going to bring him here, but he had to get in the way and look where that got him."

I silently cried.

"He might be dead already." He shrugged. He obviously didn't care either way since he wasn't even bothering to check Nathan's pulse. "And if he's not, then he will be soon." He reached out to touch my cheek. "Sorry, darling."

"How long are you going to keep me here for?" I demanded angrily.

"For as long as I'd like."

Without saying anything else, he turned and began to walk away and disappeared through the door again.

I looked down at Nathan.

He wasn't moving. He wasn't making any sound.

I took a few deep breaths as I tried to calm myself. *No he has to be alive.* I desperately needed to know if he was alive. I knew he was hurt from somewhere in his stomach. He was losing a lot of blood. *He couldn't die—not like this. Not because of me.*

I tried to concentrate on his stomach, to try to see if I would see any movement that would indicate that he was still breathing.

"Nathan," I whispered, trying to move him with my foot. It was hard because my ankles were tied to the chair but I was able to nudge his shoulder. He was close enough for me to touch him with the tip of my toe. "Nathan, please wake up." I hissed as I continued to nudge him. I didn't know how long I did this before he finally moved. He moved his shoulder and then he let out a groan. I felt a wave of relief flow through my body. I wanted to cry but I forced myself not to.

"Nathan," I said, nudging him again. "Nathan."

144

He opened his eyes and blinked for a few seconds as if trying to clear his vision. He frowned and tried to stand up. He groaned in pain as his hand went to his stomach.

"Nathan, please be quiet," I begged him as I looked around nervously.

He turned at the sound of my voice and I had never been more happy to see him than in that moment. His green eyes seemed darker than usual, his lips were chapped, and he did look pale. But he was alive and that was all that mattered.

"H-Hannah?" he asked, his voice was hoarse. "What—?" he groaned again when he tried to move.

"Nathan, they kidnapped us. We need to get out of here. Please try to be as alert as possible," I said as he clutched his abdomen. When he looked at his hand, it was filled with blood.

"He shot me," he whispered, frowning as he remembered what happened. "He—they—" he turned to look at me as if barely realizing what was happening. "Are you hurt?"

I actually half smiled. "Are you kidding? You're asking *me* if I'm hurt?"

He scanned my body and then he sat up slowly and began to untie my feet. He had lost a lot of blood and I was scared that he would pass out again. However, he was able to stand up on his feet and untied me. My hands were cold when I finally brought them to the front of my body. My shoulders ached but it felt good to be free again.

Nathan leaned against the table with a hand pressed at his abdomen. "We need to get out of here," he murmured.

He was awake, but I could tell that he wasn't fully aware of what was happening. I knew he was trying and I just hoped that it was enough for us to get out of here. I stood up, my body ached for a stretch but there was no time.

"Let me see," I said as I moved his hand away. He was sweating and wincing in pain as he moved his hand away. I ripped a piece off my long dress. The bullet had probably gone into the right side of his abdomen. There was so much blood. I grabbed the cut-out piece of cloth from my dress and wrapped it around his waist to at least stop the bleeding. "Are you okay?" I looked up at him. I knew it was a stupid question but I was just so happy that he was alive.

Nathan tried to smile. "I will be."

I nodded. "Okay."

He looked around. "We need to find anything that can help us get out of here okay? Anything that could be used as a weapon. How many of them are they?"

"I've only seen two," I answered.

He nodded as he limped around the garage. I tried to be fast so he wouldn't have to move a lot. I half ran to the cars and found some tools but nothing that seemed useful. I was shaking. I knew they could come back any minute.

"Hannah!"

I looked up and Nathan was leaning on one of the cars. "Can you get that for me?" He was pointing at something on the car seat. "I saw them put a gun in there before they knocked me out."

I reached out for the backpack and opened it. I looked inside and saw a stack of money, drugs, and a gun. Nathan took the gun and checked to see if it had bullets. That was when we heard the door open, we crouched down. He was wincing in pain and I looked away. I hated to see him in so much pain but at least he was alive.

"Hannah?" the man called. "John! Get the fuck in here!"

"Boss?" I heard John ask.

"Where the fuck is she?" the man yelled.

Nathan looked down at the gun in his hand. "I don't want you to see this."

I placed my hand on top of his. "Don't worry about me, Nathan. Do whatever you have to do."

I knew what I was telling him to do and I knew it wouldn't be easy for either of us but we had to get out of here somehow.

"I will get you out of here, Hannah."

"Hey!"

We both looked up at John who was staring at us with wide eyes. I covered my face with my hands just before I heard Nathan's gun fire.

CHAPTER 28

Two bullets. Two seconds.

That was how long it took to end this torture. The sound of the gun being fired made my ears ring.

"Hannah!" I heard Nathan call.

I was scared to open my eyes but I knew I had to. When I opened them, I saw John on the ground, motionless. The other man was also on the ground a few feet away from us but he wasn't dead. Nathan had shot him on the knee so he couldn't move.

"Run. Find a phone," Nathan ordered, not taking his eyes off the man on the ground. He had the gun pointed to his head.

I nodded as I stood up and ran to the back of the garage. I went through the mysterious door they always disappeared into and realized that it was an office. I looked through the desk with shaky hands until I finally found a phone. I dialed 911.

"My name is Hannah Collins," I said as soon as they answered. "I was kidnapped. I have no idea where I am but please send help."

"Okay, ma'am, please try to stay calm," the operator said on the phone. "Is there anyone else with you?"

I nodded. "Yes, my bodyguard. He's hurt. Please, you gotta send an ambulance quickly."

"Okay, I was able to get your location with the cell phone you're using. Our officers are on their way. Are you in a safe place right now?"

"I—one of the kidnappers is still alive. Please hurry," I said as I looked around the office. It was really messy; papers were scattered everywhere, half-eaten food, and trash on the floor. There was something on the desk that caught my eye. I reached for the delicate gold necklace that was on the laptop. It caught my eye because I had seen that necklace before. It had the same, small crystal hanging from it. It belonged to my mom. He must have stolen it. That meant he had been in our house. I put it in my pocket and then headed back to the garage.

Nathan was still pointing the gun on the man whom I still had yet to find out the name. He was on the ground, clutching at his right knee, looking at us with amusement. As if we were a part of an inside joke that Nathan and I weren't aware of.

I looked at Nathan who didn't take his eyes off of him. "Help is on the way," I said, breathless. I looked down at his abdomen and saw that he had bled through the cloth. "Oh, Nathan."

"I'm okay," he assured me but I knew he wasn't. He looked even more pale than before and he was sweating. I knew he would pass out any second and I hoped the police would arrive before then. I wanted to ask him why he didn't kill the man but I knew he wanted to know who he was. Probably wanted him to pay for this and for the massacre he had caused in Miami. At least those victims were getting justice.

I looked around the garage and noticed that there was door. I stood up and looked for a button to open it so it would be easier for the police to find us. I finally found a remote and pressed on the button to open the door. It screeched as it pulled open.

I almost cried when finally felt the fresh air. It was dark outside and I wondered how late it was. *Was my family sleeping? Had they been notified that I was okay? Were they on their way here?*

It wasn't long before I finally heard the cry of the ambulance and police cars. I walked back to Nathan. "They're here," I said as I touched his shoulder.

His arm was beginning to shake and I knew he was tired but he didn't move. He just nodded.

149

I looked at the man as red and blue lights illuminated the garage. He grinned at me. "This nightmare is far from over, darling," he promised me as officers began to flood in.

"Put your hands in the air!"

As soon as the officers came into the garage, Nathan put his arm down and allowed himself to collapse. I sat there and watched everything move in slow motion: the cops clasping the man's hands behind his back and pulling him up; his dangerous smile as he looked at me; the cops inspecting John's body on the ground; paramedics placing Nathan on a stretcher and rolling him outside.

"Is he going to be okay?" I asked the officers.

"They're going to do everything they can, miss," one of them said. "Can you please give me your name?"

"Hannah, Hannah Collins," I said as my eyes followed Nathan out of the garage.

"I got her," the officer said into a radio. "Miss, why don't we go outside? We need to ask you some questions."

I nodded quickly and followed him outside.

By then, the garage was filled with cops examining everything and it wasn't until then that I felt relief go through my body. It was over. Outside, it was cold and dark but I didn't care. I didn't think I would ever be able to go outside again. The cop had me sit down on the back of an ambulance, and a paramedic placed a blanket on my shoulders. Then she began to examine me. I couldn't tell where we were. There were a lot of cop cars and ambulances to look around my surroundings and find out, but I looked as if we were in a neighborhood.

"Ms. Collins? Are you alright?" a cop asked me.

"Can you please call my dad?" I choked out as tears ran down my cheeks. I felt like a little girl but I didn't care. I just wanted to see my dad. I wanted him to hug me and tell me that everything was going to be okay.

He nodded. "Your family has been contacted and they'll be here soon."

150

I nodded. "Okay."

"I need you to answer some questions for me, okay?"

I nodded again as the paramedic measured my blood pressure and then checked my heart.

"Did you know either of these men?"

I shook my head. "I had never seen them in my life."

"Did your bodyguard shoot that man?"

I looked at him. "It was self-defense! You can't charge him for that! He was trying to save us!" I cried.

The cop nodded. "I know, miss, I know."

I shook my head as I cried. He stopped asking questions, probably realizing that I wasn't emotionally stable for an interrogation. I didn't know how much time had passed by before I finally saw my dad. He was looking around until he spotted me. He ran to me and enveloped me in a hug, which made me cry even more. He ran his hand through my hair as he held me and I cried onto his chest.

He kept whispering, "It's okay. You're okay."

He was proof that this was over. I was going home. After pulling away, I noticed Nick and Rachel and then hugged them. My mom was also here. She was looking around, distracted.

"Where's Nathan?" Dad asked after a moment. "Did he—"

"No," I interrupted him. "He was shot, Dad, he saved me." I reached for his hand and squeezed it. "Please, he can't die. We have to go, please."

"I'll go check on him. You need to go to the hospital to get checked too," he said.

I shook my head. "I'm fine. We need to make sure Nathan is okay."

"Miss, you have an injury on the back of your head that will need a few stitches," the paramedic jumped in when my dad looked at her.

I sighed. "Fine, but take me to the same hospital they took Nathan to."

Dad nodded. "Don't worry about anything, honey. Everything will be okay."

I let the paramedic lady lead me to the stretcher they had inside the ambulance and sat down. Dad came in the ambulance with me while the rest got back in the car and said they'll meet us at the hospital. Dad held me as the ambulance drove off. It wasn't long before my eyes closed involuntarily and I fell into a restless sleep.

~

Two days. We had been there for two days.

It felt like an eternity but it had only been two days.

The police informed my dad that the name of the other kidnapper was Steven Powell. He was a salesman and he had no family except for John who was his cousin. John had been previously suspected of using his business as cover for selling drugs and after what they found, they confirmed those suspicions. They were yet to find the reason Steve did this to me.

I was in the hospital with needles connected to an IV. My vision had finally cleared up but I still felt exhausted and a bit disoriented. Mom and dad were in the room, together with Colton and my little brother, Derek.

"Hannah, how are you feeling?" Dad asked after the doctor had checked up on me.

"Better," I said. "How's Nathan? Is he okay?"

"They had to do a surgery to take out the bullet but he's already out of surgery and in recovery. The doctors said he's going to be just fine. He just needs to rest for next few weeks."

I wanted to ask Dad if Nathan was already awake and if I could see him but I didn't. He was going to be okay; that's all that mattered right now.

"Thank God, you're okay, Hannah."

I half smiled at my brother, Derek. "You're really here."

I hadn't seen him in so long. It was so good to have him here with me. Derek was tall with a fit body. He had short brown

152

hair and blue eyes. He had a perfect nose, jaw, and a good face. He was a model for a reason.

"Of course, I am," he said as he leaned in to kiss my cheek.

It was a miracle. My family was complete. Mom was sitting on the couch going through a magazine. Nick and Colton were chatting suspiciously about something and Rachel was sitting next to me, reading a book.

Dad reached for my hand. "I've never felt so useless in my life. I'm so sorry sweetie."

"Dad, it's okay," I said, trying to comfort him. "I'm okay. Thanks to Nathan."

Dad nodded. "I owe him for life."

"Do you think I can see him now?" I asked, trying to sound casual.

Rachel looked up at me curiously. She had secretly been giving me more updates. Apparently, Jared came to see Nathan which made me feel slightly better. At least he wasn't alone.

Dad frowned. "I don't think that's a good idea."

I reached for his hand and squeezed it. "Dad, please, I just want to see him and make sure he's okay. I owe him that much and more."

He studied me. "I'll go get the nurse."

I smiled. "Thank you."

"Yeah, yeah," he said then turned and walked out of the room.

I looked at Rachel and she winked at me.

Dad came back minutes later with a nurse and a wheelchair. I thought it wasn't necessary but he helped me onto the wheelchair and then pushed me down the hall. Nathan's room was only a few doors down from mine. I noticed that bodyguards filled the hospital hallway which meant my dad was still a little uneasy. When my dad pushed me into Nathan's room and I saw Nathan, I wanted to burst into tears. He looked so pale. His cheeks were swollen and bruised. He had a tube that went into his nose, to help him breathe. His eyes were closed. He wasn't moving. His skin was as white as paper.

"Nathan," I whispered as I wheeled closer to him. "Are you sure he's going to be okay?" I asked my dad.

"The doctors assured me he would be," my dad said behind me. "Of course, he'll need a lot of rest and won't be able to work for a while. If he still wanted to work…" his voice trailed off.

I sat there in silence for a moment, wishing my dad would get out so I could kiss him. I wanted to say so many things to him. I wanted to tell him that I was sorry—he was here because of me.

But most of all, I wanted to apologize because I hadn't been brave enough to tell my dad or anyone what he really meant to me. I didn't know why but I couldn't bring myself to tell my dad the truth.

I wasn't brave enough. I knew it like I knew that I didn't deserve Nathan.

CHAPTER 29

Three months later

I checked the time on my phone. 12:23 pm.

I frowned. I had a class at one.

With a sigh, I shut the book in my hands and jumped out of bed. I began to pack everything in my backpack then grabbed my sweater and headed downstairs.

It had been about three months since the kidnapping and the scars around my wrists and ankles were still visible. They were faint scars but one look at them and everything came rushing back in.

It had been all over the news.

Everywhere.

Every time I turned the TV on or checked social media—they were talking about me, the poor daughter of Richard Collins. Cameras began to flood my family again and they were barely beginning to leave us alone.

The problem was that it wasn't the kidnapping that hurt—it was Nathan. I hadn't seen him since the last time I saw him in the hospital. I tried to see him but something always seemed to get in the way. First, my dad wouldn't get off my back. He would watch me every second of the day. When he wasn't there, Nick or Colton would took over. It was great to have my brothers around for a change but not when I was trying to sneak out. When I finally did sneak out, two weeks after, it was too late. Nathan was already out of the hospital.

I was desperate.

I didn't have any other way to contact him. I tried going to his apartment but no one had answered. When I asked Robin about him, he said the only thing he knew was that a friend had helped Nathan out which meant that he must have gone home with Jared.

I knew it was my fault. I knew I should have just told my parents the truth, but I couldn't.

On the other hand, everything was finally looking up with my relationship with my mom. She had been paying me more attention. Asking how my dad was and being less hard on me. I didn't want to mess this up by telling her about Nathan.

I hated myself for it.

I knew that if I couldn't put Nathan before my parents— then I didn't deserve him. He was an honorable man. After everything he did for me, he didn't deserve how I was treating him. I should have stood up for *us* and told my parents about us but I didn't. And now it was too late. Nathan was gone.

I didn't know if he was coming back. I figured he wouldn't want to do anything with me after everything he went through because of me. That was the problem. After everything he went through because of me, the least I could have done was stood by his side and told my parents about us when I had the chance at the hospital.

But I was a coward.

"Hannah!"

I stopped in my tracks when I heard Rachel call me. I walked a few steps back and realized she had called me from the kitchen.

"Come!" she whispered, waving at me.

I frowned. "Rachel, what are you doing?" I asked as I walked into the kitchen.

"Guess what Nick just told me?" she asked.

It was about to be lunch time so the maids were preparing lunch behind her. Rachel had an apron on and I realized she was helping them. Sometimes she did that.

"Rachel, I have class in less than an hour—"

"Nathan's coming back," she interrupted me.

"What?"

She nodded with a smile. "Nick just told me that Richard told that Nathan had called and said that he was well and ready to work."

I gulped. "Why would he want to be back?" I asked stupidly.

"Richard wondered the same thing. He didn't think Nathan would to come back after what happened."

"When?" I asked. My mind was working rapidly, trying to chew on the fact that I would actually see Nathan again.

"Tomorrow," Rachel answered, placing her hands on my shoulders. "He's coming back, Hannah."

"He's coming back," I repeated.

There was suddenly a knot in my throat.

"Hannah?" Rachel asked, bringing me back to reality.

"I—have to go. I have class," I said quickly and then turned around and half ran out of the house.

Jack, my bodyguard while Nathan wasn't around, opened the car door for me and I hopped in. The ride to school was quiet and when we got there, I suddenly didn't feel like staying. I couldn't stop thinking about Nathan, about seeing him again. My chest tightened just by thinking about it. I missed him so much…

I felt a cold, gentle breeze that made me glad I had worn my sweater despite it being a sunny day. It was mid-March so the weather wasn't as bad as in January.

I walked to class, feeling numb. I couldn't concentrate and by the time it was over, I realized I had no idea what it the class was about. I knew Jack was waiting but I still took my time. I went to get a coffee and took my time walking back to the car while still thinking about Nathan. In less than twenty-four hours, I would see him again.

Would he still be my bodyguard?

If he had decided to come back, then it must mean that he didn't hate me.

I walked back to the car and by the time I got home, it was already time for dinner.

I was going to have dinner with just my parents tonight since Rachel and Nick had stayed out working late.

"Is everything alright, Hannah?"

I looked up at my mom who was frowning at me. "Yeah, just tired."

"You haven't touched your food." She noted, looking at my plate.

I picked up the fork and began to cut a piece of the breaded chicken and put it in my mouth.

"I haven't told you—" my dad said. "—Nathan called. He'll be back tomorrow."

I felt my body began to shake just at the sound of his name. "He is?" I asked quietly as I picked at my food.

My dad nodded. "Yes. To be honest, I didn't expect him to come back. But he insisted."

"Hmm," I murmured as I tried to eat. After a moment, I stood up. "Um—I'm going to sleep now. I'm really tired." I tried to smile at them. "Good night."

"Good night, honey," I heard my dad say before I walked out of the dining room. I rushed to my room. I was so nervous about seeing him again that I found myself throwing up three times during the night.

When morning came, I watched the sun rise from my toilet. I dragged my body to the bath and took the longest shower I had ever taken.

I thought about him. About the times when we were together. About the times we spent together in the car on our way to Miami. Those memories felt like a movie playing back in my head.

I was driving myself crazy.

I decided I wasn't going to go out of my room for the entire day. It was Saturday so I didn't have school. So I hid in my room all day, like the coward I was. Thankfully, nobody bothered me.

At around six, I got a text from Rachel.

Hannah, can you go in my room and check if I unplugged the iron? I'm sorry, I forgot and I don't want to burn down the house lol

I rolled my eyes at her text. Rachel was always forgetting something.

With a sigh, I stood up and opened the door slowly. Rachel's room was just two doors down from mine and there was no one in the hallway so I ran to her room. I closed the door quietly behind me and then walked straight into the bathroom which was the first thing I saw to my left.

I didn't see the iron so I walked out of the bathroom and made my way to the main room. I found the iron in her closet and it was unplugged.

I was texting her, telling her it had been unplugged when the door suddenly opened. I felt my throat dry up when I saw *him* walk in.

Nathan's eyes widened when he saw me, he looked just as surprised.

He was here.

In front of me.

The one person I was dying to see but had been avoiding all day.

CHAPTER 30

Nathan and I stared at each other for what seemed like forever. Shockingly enough, he looked the same. He was wearing his usual black suit with white shirt, black tie, and black shoes to match. His hair was pulled back and his face looked clean. I could tell he recently had shaven.

The fact that there was no apparent trace of what happened on his face made me realize that enough time had passed. Enough time had passed for his wounds to heal, for the bruises to fade.

Too much time had passed.

"I—" he hesitated, "—I'm sorry. I didn't know you were here. Rachel." He stopped as we both realized what Rachel had done.

I didn't know whether I loved her or hated her right now.

There was a coldness in Nathan's voice that made my chest tighten.

"I'm glad you're okay," I said after a moment.

He frowned. "Are you?"

"Of course, I am."

He crossed his arms in his chest, making him look even more intimidating. "You have a funny way of showing it."

He was glaring at me. He was angry. He had every right to be. I wasn't ready for this. I wanted the earth to swallow me. I didn't think it was possible to feel even more horrible than I already did. The knot in my throat was threatening to make me cry any second.

"I'm sorry," I whispered.

"For what?" he asked, looking at me.

I looked away for a moment. There were so many things I was sorry for. There were so many things I wanted to tell him...yet not a single word came out of my mouth.

I hated the distance between us. He hadn't moved from the door and he had made no indication that he wanted to be closer to me. If he weren't blocking the only way out, I would have already ran out. He was so close yet so far. I felt a tear roll down my cheek and I wiped it quickly.

"*Everything*," I finally said.

And then I let out a sob and began to cry. I watched Nathan take a step forward but I raised my palm at him. "Don't." I cried and then covered my face with my hands.

He stayed where he was while I tried to compose myself.

"I wanted to see you—" I began after I stopped crying. "I did but I couldn't."

"Why?" he asked, dropping his hands to his sides.

I sniffed. "I couldn't bring myself to tell my parents about us. And when I was able to sneak out, you weren't in the hospital anymore. I didn't know how to find you."

He took a step forward. "When I woke up on that hospital bed, the only person I wanted to see was *you*...but you were gone."

His words were making me feel even worse. The tears kept rolling down my cheeks and I wiped them out with my hand over and over again.

"I'm sorry," I said again. "You must regret saving my life."

He shook his head and his eyes softened. "I knew you and I weren't exclusive, Hannah. I knew that we never made anything official..." he continued after a moment. "...but you are special to me. I would never regret saving you. It is the one thing in my life I have done right."

"I feel horrible—" I sniffed, "—for not being with you." My voice cracked in the end and I cried for a moment. Nathan crossed the distance between us but I took a step back and raised my palm again, stopping him. "Please," I said looking up at him. "Let me finish."

He nodded as he looked at me with a worried expression on his face. It felt so good to see his green eyes again...to have him this close that I could smell him.

"I wanted to tell my parents. Please believe me," I said.

"I do," he said softly.

I shook my head. "But *I couldn't*—so many things were going on at once and I'm not trying to make up excuses." I looked up at him. "I am eternally grateful to you, Nathan. Even if I haven't done a good job on showing it, I am so thankful. *You saved my life*," I sniffed. "I wanted to tell them," I repeated. "I *wanted* to. It was the least I could do after everything you did for me."

"Please stop crying, Hannah," he said. "It's breaking my heart to see you like this."

"I can't," I said, half laughing and half crying.

My eyes felt swollen and I felt my face flushed.

"I thought I was never going to see you again." I shook my head as the tears continued to roll down my cheeks. "And that would have sucked because I think I've fallen in love with you." I covered my face with hands again as I broke down crying for the hundredth time since I saw him.

This time, Nathan walked to me and put his arms around me and held me close to him. I felt home again when I buried my face in his chest. He was holding me tight and I was glad because I was sure I would have fallen if it weren't for him. My knees felt weak as I tried to control myself.

After a while, I finally stopped crying. Nathan kept holding me and I wrapped my arms around his torso and closed my eyes.

I had done it.

I had said it to him.

The thing that I had been trying to so hard to ignore was that *I loved him*. The more I thought about it, the more sure I was. I had fallen in love with my bodyguard.

162

After a moment, Nathan pulled away and placed his hands on each of my cheeks. His cold hands felt good against my flushed skin.

He half smiled. "That's not fair. I wanted to be the first one to say it."

I smiled. "You still can," I said, my voice a little croaky.

"I've known for a while now. I've known since the day we spent together in the woods, do you remember?"

I nodded, smiling. "Of course."

"I love your eyes," he said, looking at me. "I love the way you laugh. I love your smile. I love your lips." He ran his thumb against them. "I love that you are not afraid to eat in front of me— even if sometimes I do think you eat too much," he said, making me laugh. "I love your hair, your skin," he paused. "I love *you*, Hannah. I've known it for a while now and I regret not telling you sooner."

"You're going to make me cry again," I complained. The knot in my throat was still there. The last time I cried like this was in that garage when I thought Nathan was dead. But he wasn't. He was here, with me and he loved me.

He shook his head. "No, please don't," he said, wiping the tear that escaped.

I smiled. "It's okay, they're happy tears."

"I came back for you, Hannah." He smiled. "Jared didn't want me to come back. He told me I had risked my life too much, but *I had to* come back. I had to see you. I had to tell you how much I love you." His hand lowered down to my waist and then he reached down and placed his lips on mine.

I closed my eyes, enjoying this moment. I thought I was never going to feel his lips again.

He began to kiss me, slowly.

"I love you," he whispered against my lips. "I love you so much. My Hannah. My beautiful Hannah."

CHAPTER 31

Nathan held me in his arms for the longest moment. His hug was mending everything broken in me. It was exactly what I needed. Even after coming home from the hospital, I still didn't feel complete. It didn't feel right to come home without him. It didn't feel right that I hadn't seen him or spoken to him after what happened. I went on pretending that I was fine but I wasn't. I loved Nathan and I didn't want to be without him anymore.

I thought I had lost him and but didn't. Now, he was here with me and he was holding me tight and I finally felt that hole in my chest be filled. I was starting to feel like myself again.

"We should probably get out of Rachel's room," I finally broke the silence.

Nathan's chest vibrated under my cheek as he chuckled. "I guess we should."

I pulled away but reached for his hand. "Come on," I said then pulled him out of the room. I checked the hallways first and then pulled him into my room. I locked the door behind me.

"I'm supposed to be on duty," Nathan said, looking at me with an amused expression on his face.

"Technically, you are under my service," I said, making him laugh. I smiled at him. "Lay with me?"

"Well, *you are* my boss..." He grinned.

I smiled then lay on the bed. Nathan lay next to me, putting an arm around my shoulders and pressing himself closer to me.

"I missed you," I whispered.

Nathan kissed my cheek. "I missed you too. You were all I thought about for the past months."

I turned my head so that I could look at him. "Where did you go? After they cleared you at the hospital?"

"With my friend Jared." He looked at me. "He and Jenny, his wife, helped me get better."

I looked away, feeling sad again. It should have been me.

I turned so that I was lying on my side. Nathan's arm went around my waist and I felt him kiss the crook of my neck. "You should sleep," he whispered.

I closed my heavy eyes, I was tired but I didn't want to sleep. I missed him so much and he was here, I didn't want to waste any second.

"I'm not going anywhere, Hannah," he said as if reading my mind.

I smiled. "Okay."

I tried not to sleep right away but falling asleep was easy when I was safe in Nathan's arms.

The next morning, a knock on the door woke me up and I noticed that I was alone in my bed as soon as I opened my eyes.

So much for not going anywhere, I thought as the door opened.

"Hannah."

I blinked a few times. "Mom?"

"Good, you're awake." She walked to the windows and pulling the curtains open. Bright light came into the room, making my eyes hurt. "We're going to go to Sandy's for breakfast. Hurry up and change," she said then walked out.

I groaned. Sandy's was my dad's favorite breakfast restaurant. We had been going there for years. It had become quite known though because the cameras had followed us the last time we went there.

I didn't really want to go but I didn't want to stay in the house alone either. So, I got out bed and took a shower. I brushed my teeth, combed my hair, and changed into jeans and a green sweater, and put on my black and white Vans. As I walked down the stairs, I immediately searched for Nathan.

"Hannah, come on," my mom urged when she saw me.

I followed her outside and smiled when I saw *him*. He was opening the door for us; my dad was already inside the car.

"Rachel and Nick are meeting us there," my mom said as the car started and pulled out of the driveway.

"Why are we going there?" I asked her.

The smile on her lips fell short. "Your dad is starting to shoot another film this week so he'll be gone for a while."

I bit my lip. I knew she didn't like it whenever my dad had to leave to shoot for a film. I didn't like it much either because he was always gone for months though I hoped it would be different now that my mom and I were getting along. Before when my dad would leave, it would put my mom in a bad mood and she would be colder to me than usual. It was hell. I turned around and looked through the tinted window of our car. I could see a black car following us. I knew the media would follow us. They were still trying to get a story out of my dad about what had happened to me and Nick despite the fact that it had been all over the news already. Why couldn't they just let us be in peace? I sighed as I leaned my head back and thought about Nathan who was sitting in the passenger seat. I wanted to tell my parents about him. The reason that I couldn't do it before was because he wasn't with me. I needed him then to give me the courage…and now he was finally with me.

I felt so happy. I hadn't felt this happy in ages. Nathan was a dream come true.

When we reached the restaurant, we got out of the car and went in without a problem. We sat at our usual booth. The owner had known us for years; since before my dad became famous. It was a small restaurant but it was really homey. The owners were really friendly and so were the employees. They had to smile all the time; it must be a requirement if they wanted to work here.

"By the way," I said to Rachel as I reached for my glass of water. "I know what you did yesterday."

She smiled mischievously. "I'm sorry but both of you were being stubborn. And I love playing cupid." She clapped her hands silently.

My parents and Nick were in a deep conversation that they weren't even paying attention to us. I could see Nathan standing by the doorway with two other bodyguards.

I rolled my eyes at her. "Well, thank you."

She smiled, looking very content with herself. "Does that mean everything went well?"

"It didn't start out very good," I admitted then smiled. "But I love him Rachel and he loves me." I sighed. "You have no idea how happy I am."

"Good. You deserve it." She glanced at my parents who sat across from us. "When are you telling them?"

"I don't know," I said, suddenly feeling nervous. "I'm a little scared to be honest."

She smiled. "No kidding."

"But I want to do it. I *need* to do it."

"I'm sure it'll be okay, Hannah." She assured me as our server approached us.

We ordered and then chatted while waiting for our orders.

"I have a fashion show in two months," Rachel said when the food finally arrived. "You have to come."

I nodded. "You know I don't miss them."

I loved going to Rachel's fashion shows. I generally liked fashion shows but Rachel's were extra special. I loved seeing her collection come to life and I loved being there for her. She had turned into the sister I never had.

Martha, the owner, joined us as we were finishing breakfast and it was a while before my dad was ready to go since he was in a deep conversation with her.

When we finally headed outside groups of paparazzi and reporters were waiting for us with their cameras. They were still a

167

little hyped up because the investigation was still ongoing. Steve Powell had denied Nick's attack and he wasn't confessing to my kidnapping or attack in Miami. Through my dad's lawyers, I knew that he had requested to speak with me. That was his condition to talk. Maybe it was selfish, but I had no desire in speaking with him and I refused to do so from the moment my dad told me about Steve's intentions. What did he want to speak to me about anyway? He would just torment me more. There was enough proof to charge him for my kidnapping but his confession about Miami and Nick's attack was needed since there was nothing that related him to those incidents, except my declaration about what he told me back in that garage and even then he had said nothing about Nick. He had probably gotten rid of the weapons and John was dead so there wasn't much that the investigators could do.

There was something about the whole situation that was making me uneasy. I couldn't forget the words he had told me that day. *This nightmare is far from over.* And then there was my mom's necklace. I wanted to know how he had gotten it. My guess was that he broke into the house but why did he only take that specific piece of jewelry? He could have taken something else. I also wondered how he was able to get in the house so easily without any of the bodyguards catching him. I hated to think of it but it sounded like an inside job. I was starting to think that maybe speaking with him wouldn't be the worst thing in the world. I could get answers to my questions. It would end this investigation, and I could get the closure I needed.

Rachel and I walked behind everyone else and I could feel Nathan close behind me. I looked down at my feet as I walked to avoid the flashing from the cameras. We had almost made it to the car when one of the paparazzi got a hold of my arm, and pulled me to him. He began to shout questions at me, as if he hadn't just tried to pull my arm off.

"Let her go," Nathan warned, standing protectively next to me.

168

I tried to pull my arm away from the paparazzi's his grip but he had a tight hold on my arm. I didn't know what he was trying to accomplish with this. I wasn't even answering any of his questions.

"Come on, man. I just have a few questions?" he said, still holding my arm. He turned to look at me and smirked. "Who is he? Is he your boyfriend?"

"Let her go, mate," Nathan repeated, he was glaring at him and I was scared of what he was going to do if he didn't let me go.

I glanced at my parents who had stopped by the car and were glancing over at us. I opened my mouth but before I could say anything, Nathan placed his hand on the man's shoulder and shoved him over to the side. My mouth opened in shock when I saw the camera hit the ground, some parts of it flying out.

Nathan took a step forward. I grabbed his arm. "Nathan, don't. Please..." I begged in a low voice.

Everyone was taking pictures. The man was still on the ground, looking scared as he looked up at Nathan.

I pulled Nathan's arm. "Come on."

I was surprised but he actually turned around. My parents got in the car and I got in after them.

"What was that about?" my mom asked, looking at Nathan from the backseat.

"Christina, he was just protecting Hannah," my dad said.

I rubbed my arm. I wasn't trying to be dramatic, it really did ache.

"I hate them," I murmured.

"Well, we are lucky no one really got seriously hurt," my mom said. "That could have turned into an assault. You should be more careful in dealing with the media, Nathan. We could be sued," she scolded.

"Mom—" I turned to look at her. "Are you kidding? You're mad at him for defending me?"

She looked at me. "I'm just saying that he may have overreacted a little."

169

I looked at my dad and rolled my eyes then turned around and looked out the window. This had only made me more nervous. My mom seemed to have changed but I knew she hadn't turned into the perfect mother overnight. I knew she wasn't going to like it when I told her about Nathan and me. The thought tormented me all the way home.

CHAPTER 32

When we got home, my parents got out of the car and I pretended to be on my phone while they walked into the house. Nathan walked into view with his hands in his pockets.

I got out of the car and looked up at him. "I'm starting to think you have anger issues."

He chuckled. "I will not apologize. He was an ass handling you like that."

I moved my head to the side with a smile. "He was. Thank you."

His green eyes looked amused. "Don't you think I deserve a kiss?"

I nodded, bringing my eyebrows together. "Maybe, yes."

He grinned at me. "I'm waiting."

I looked around, there were bodyguards everywhere. I could even see the gardener trimming the bushes. "Right now?"

He took a step towards me. "Come with me," he said then turned around.

Making sure no member of my family was in sight, I followed him. He went through the backdoor of the house. We passed the kitchen, down to a hallway I had only been once before we moved into the house. The hallway had doors on each sides and Nathan opened one and grabbed my hand and pulled me in. It was a small room with a bunk bed and two drawers. It had a TV and I could see the bathroom. I recognized the black tie and white shirt by the corner.

Nathan's hand snaked around my waist and he pulled me to him, crashing his lips against mine. I found myself taking a few steps back until I felt the wall behind me.

"Whoa," I whispered, breathless after the hot make out session with Nathan.

He grinned as I felt his hand drop down below my waist, he placed it on my butt and gave it a little squeeze.

I started to laugh. "Nathan!" I hissed trying to be quiet.

He chuckled at the expression in my face. "What? You have a really nice ass, Collins."

"Stop it!" I said, feeling my face get hot.

He laughed but his hand went back on my waist. He picked me up and I wrapped my legs around his torso as I leaned against the wall. I was finally as tall as him.

He looked at me for a moment.

"What?" I asked him. He was starting to make me feel self-conscious.

"I can't stare at my beautiful girlfriend?"

I felt a warm feeling in my stomach and I couldn't help but smile. "I'm sorry, I don't remember anyone asking me if I wanted to be their girlfriend."

"Hannah Collins—"

"Nathan—" I frowned. "What's your last name?"

He chuckled. "Hayes."

"Nathan Hayes." *Hannah Hayes, I liked it.*

He leaned in and planted a kiss on my lips. "Please be my girlfriend," he whispered against my lips.

I smiled. "Of course." I kissed him.

He began to kiss my neck and then I felt his lips on my ear. "Now, I would like to make love to my girlfriend," he whispered seductively.

His voice alone was the sexiest thing ever.

Please do.

My hands wrapped around his neck as he began to walk us to the bed. He placed me down gently, and then straighten up, hitting his head on the bed on top.

He chuckled. "Ow."

I couldn't stop laughing. "I'm sorry. Are you okay?" I asked, looking up at him.

"You're going to be sorry you laughed," he teased, taking off his jacket and then his tie. I watched as he stripped down in front of me. I pulled my sweater over my head and unbuttoned my jeans, pulling them down and then kicking them off with my feet. He leaned down and began to kiss my stomach, sending fireworks all over my body. He placed his big hands on my thighs as he worked his way up. He pulled my panties down and I felt him work his way inside of me, making me throw my head back. He began to kiss my neck with urgency.

"I love you Hannah," he whispered against my lips as he moved on top of me. "I love you more than anything in this world." His green eyes were a darker shade as he looked at me.

A quiet moan escaped from my throat. I wanted to tell him that I loved him too but I couldn't speak. I couldn't concentrate on anything else except for how good he was making me feel.

I felt *wanted*. I felt *loved*.

"*I love you,*" Nathan whispered over and over as he made me his once more.

~

Nathan and I got in the shower afterwards. It started to become a habit for us. I didn't even care that my hair was still wet from the shower I took in the morning. Showers with Nathan were something I wouldn't miss for the world.

"My dad is leaving soon," I said as I used Nathan's comb to comb my hair. I turned to look at him. He was putting on his white shirt and I watched as he buttoned it. "I want to tell him before he leaves."

He nodded as he tucked in his shirt and put on his belt. "We can go right now."

I looked up at him. "Really?"

"Yeah."

"You're not nervous?" *Cause I was.*

He half smiled. "Of course, but I want him to know that I am serious about our relationship. I don't want to hide it." He put the black tie around his neck.

I smiled as I stood up. "Let me," I said, reaching up. I put his tie underneath his collar and began to tie it.

"How did you learn to do this?" Nathan asked me.

"I have three brothers. Two of whom own nothing but suits. They would sleep in them if they could."

"Well, we already have something in common." He winked at me.

I smiled at him as I finished. "You're serious about this?"

"Of course, I am." He kissed my forehead. "I want to be able to take you out on dates without worrying."

I bit my lip. "Even if you lose your job?"

He looked down at me and placed his hand on my cheek. "Hannah, you are so much worth than a job. Besides, given that we are in a relationship, I don't think it would be a wise thing for me to keep working for your father."

"Why not? I don't want you to stop being my bodyguard," I admitted.

I think that was the best part about our little secret. I got to have a bodyguard and a boyfriend at the same time. I knew that was going to change the moment we told my dad.

He smiled. "Believe me, I am not thrilled about getting replaced." He kissed the tip of my nose. "But I don't want him to think I'm with you for my own personal interest. I just wouldn't feel comfortable, love."

I felt like I was melting in his arms. "What did you call me?" I whispered with a smile.

Nathan smiled when he looked at me. "Love. *My* love." He kissed me.

"Okay," I whispered. I would agree to anything he told me if he called me love.

"It'll be okay," Nathan said.

I nodded.

"How have you been by the way?" he asked as he leaned on the doorway with his hands in his pockets. "You know after…"

I looked at him. "I had nightmares for the first few nights after leaving the hospital. I didn't go out for while either. My professors had to make an exception and allow me to do my work online," I admitted. "But it's better now that you're here again with me." I smiled at him.

Nathan smiled at me. "If I could do anything to change what you went through, I would."

"I wouldn't," I said. "Because you were with me. I feel like going through that, thinking you weren't going to make it, helped me realize that I wanted to be with you."

He smiled sheepishly. "Well, in that case…" he walked to me and kissed me.

"Do you know what will happen to Steve?" I asked him after a moment.

"I think he's still on trial," he said. "Why?"

I shrugged. "I don't know." I hesitated then looked up at him. "When I went into the office to find a phone, I found a gold necklace that belonged to my mom."

Nathan frowned. "Are you sure it was your mom's?"

I nodded. "It's a pretty unique necklace. He must have stolen it."

"He must have…" Nathan nodded, looking miles away.

I reached out and touched his cheek. "Would you mind being my bodyguard for just a little while after we tell my dad? I really like having you around all the time."

He grinned as he put his arms around me. "You can try to convince me…"

I laughed as I got on my tiptoes and pressed my lips to his neck, just next to his Adam's apple. I kissed his cheek and then his lips slowly. "Please?" I asked against his lips.

He smiled. "I'll think about it."

I opened my eyes and shook my head at him. "Hope you choose wisely, Hayes."

He chuckled as he followed me out of the room. In the kitchen, the cooks were already preparing lunch and I smiled at them awkwardly when they saw me with Nathan. It didn't matter anymore because pretty soon everyone was going to know.

"Wait here," I told Nathan when we stopped outside my dad's office.

I took a deep breath and knocked then opened it.

My dad looked up from his computer. "Everything okay?"

I nodded. "Yeah. Are you busy? I wanted to tell you something."

He closed his laptop and stood up. "I'm not. What is it Hannah?"

I looked at him nervously. "I wanted to—uh—" I sighed as I looked at him. "Please be okay with this," I said then turned around and went to get Nathan. I grabbed his hand and we walked into my father's office, hand in hand.

CHAPTER 33

Richard looked confused as Hannah and I walked into his office. I thought back to the last time I was in this room—back when he assigned me to protect his daughter. Now I was here to tell him I loved his daughter and to ask for his permission to date her. I was trying to be brave—Hannah was already nervous enough for both of us—but it was impossible not to feel nervous. This was the first time I was standing before the father of the girl I loved. I hadn't done this before—my past relationships were never serious enough and I never felt the need to be.

But this time was different.

I loved Hannah and I wanted her for as long as she had me.

"Nathan?" Richard looked at Hannah. "Hannah, what is going on?"

"Dad, Nathan and I have been sort of seeing each other," she said slowly.

"I don't understand," Richard said but by the way he looked at me, I could tell he knew exactly what she meant.

I took a step forward. "Richard, I love Hannah. I fell in love with her and I would like to make her my girlfriend."

Hannah was already my girlfriend—whether Richard approved or not—*she was mine.*

Richard's approval was important, of course, but I had already convinced myself that I wasn't going to let Hannah go, no way. He would have to kill me, but he wasn't a murderer so I felt pretty confident.

177

"Since when?" Richard asked his daughter.

"Uh—since Miami."

"And you kept it a secret," Richard said.

"It wasn't an appropriate relationship," Hannah said the obvious. "Besides, we hadn't really figured everything out. We just liked each other back then."

Richard walked around the table and then leaned against it with his hands in his pockets as he studied us. "And you two are completely sure?"

"Dad, we are not getting married," Hannah said.

Yet.

She looked at me and smiled. "We want to date, get to know each other better. Be together without hiding." She looked at him again. "Is that bad?"

Richard looked at her for a moment. "No, it's not." He paused. "Let me speak to Nathan."

"What? No," Hannah said quickly. Her expression made me want to laugh but I pursed my lips. Was there anything about her that I didn't love?

"I think I know better than to punch someone bigger than me," Richard said with a smile.

Hannah laughed but I could tell she was nervous. She turned to look at me. I smiled. "It's okay," I told her.

She bit her lip. Did she not realize what she was doing to me whenever she did that? It was the biggest turn on.

"Okay," she finally said then turned around and walked out, closing the door behind her.

I looked at Richard. Many people would give anything to stand before the famous actor but I found myself becoming impatient.

He took a deep breath as he looked at me. "I guess that I'm not surprised. There has always been a special way with how you have always protected Hannah. She is alive thanks to you and I will always be grateful to you for that."

I nodded. "Hannah has always been special to me, sir. I know I have broken a lot of rules and I am here to take full responsibility for that."

"That's honorable." He half-smiled. "Hannah is an adult. I know she is free to date whoever she likes. Frankly, I would like to thank *you* for coming to talk to me. She is my only daughter and it has always been important to me that she is happy with someone good for her." He studied me for a moment. "I think you are good for her, Nathan."

I smiled, feeling relief go through my body. "Thank you, sir."

"How serious are you about this?" he asked me.

"I have never been so serious about anything in my life," I paused. "I would like to date her and marry her one day if she'll have me."

He half-smiled. "You also realize you cannot continue to be her bodyguard?"

I nodded again. "I wanted to talk to you about that."

"I'm listening."

"I wanted to keep working here—just for a little while, until I find a job somewhere else."

Richard frowned. "That's not really necessary. I could promote you, Nathan."

I shook my head. "I appreciate it, sir, but I can find a job on my own."

He smiled. "If that's what you want."

"It is," I said, feeling my shoulders relaxed.

As much as I hated the idea of not being Hannah's bodyguard anymore, I knew I had to get another job. I didn't want to depend on her father. I was capable of getting a job on my own and I already had an idea.

"And I need some time to find someone to replace you. Any suggestions?" he asked, looking at me.

"Robin is really good at his job," I suggested.

I also knew he would respect Hannah.

179

Richard nodded. "I will take that into consideration. I will be out for a few weeks but I will leave everything ready for when you are ready to leave."

"Thank you so much, Mr. Collins."

"Richard." He half smiled. "If you are going to be my daughter's boyfriend, I think it's time for you to call me Richard."

I smiled. "Thank you, Richard."

"I trust you, Nathan, and I know that you will take care of her."

"I will," I promised.

He flashed a crooked grin. "Now we have to do something dangerous," he said, making his way out of the office. "We have to tell my wife."

He chuckled but I didn't find it funny at all. Christina Collins was not the easiest person to please, and I knew she wasn't going to take the news well.

We found Hannah in the kitchen, sitting at the counter, eating a cupcake. I could tell she was nervous and the sight of her stuffing a cupcake in her mouth made me want to laugh. She had frostings on the side of her mouth and I slid my tongue on my lower lip to keep myself from grabbing her and cleaning it myself. I couldn't do that in front of her father.

"What happened?" she asked as she stood up, cleaning off the frosting with a napkin.

Well, damn.

I noticed she had changed into black jeans with a red sweater. She really did look good in red. She had pulled her hair up in a nigh ponytail, exposing her beautiful neck.

"We have to tell your mother," Richard told her.

She frowned. "Can't we just let her find out through those gossip shows she watches or something?"

"*Hannah,*" Richard scolded but he was smiling as he shook his head. "I'll go get her," he said then turned around and walked out of the kitchen.

"What happened?" Hannah asked me as we walked to the living room.

"I think it went well."

She raised her eyebrows. "And?"

I grinned. "And I'll be around for a little while."

She smiled then reached up and placed a kiss on my lips. They tasted sweet and they were soft against mine. Kissing her was one of the best things to do in this world.

"Hannah?"

We pulled apart and looked up.

Nicholas and Rachel were walking down the stairs. Nick didn't have a pleased look on his face but he didn't look angry. Rachel grabbed him by his arm and pulled him back as he approached us. At the same time, Richard and Christina were walking in through the front door.

Okay, I guess it was better they found out altogether.

"What is going on?" Christina asked looking around.

"Christina, Nathan has asked for my consent to make Hannah his girlfriend," Richard said.

Hannah's arm went around mine. Her touch comforted me.

"What?" Christina asked in disbelief. She was glaring at me. "He is an *employee*." She glared at Hannah. "You chose him over George?" Her voice got louder by every word that came out of her mouth.

Hannah shook her head. "George? Mom, I love Nathan."

I looked down at her and smiled then looked at Mrs. Collins. "Ma'am, I love your daughter and I would love for you to be on board with us."

She shook her head. "No." She grabbed Hannah by the shoulders and pulled her away from me. "Hannah, I want you to have a good future—"

"And I can't have it with Nathan?"

Christina's blue eyes pierced through Hannah. "He is not the kind of man I want for you," she said slowly.

181

Hannah took a step back. "Well, I am sorry, Mom, but I am not going to leave Nathan just because he doesn't meet your expectations. I am staying with him," she said, taking a step back next to me.

"Christina, Hannah is an adult. She can be with whoever she wants," Richard said softly and Nick nodded in agreement.

Christina kept shaking her head. "I can't believe you're throwing away your future like this!" she said to Hannah. "I can't believe this!" she said, slapping her hands on her sides. "I can't believe it!" She turned around and stormed out the door.

"I apologize for my wife," Richard said. "She takes social status very seriously." He frowned at that. I'll go talk to her." He turned around and followed his wife.

"So you love my sister, eh?" Nick asked, walking in front of me.

"I do," I said, proud of how brave I sounded.

"Well, I know you didn't ask me but you have my approval," Rachel said, standing next to Nick.

Hannah laughed, and I laughed too because her laugh was contagious. It also made relief flow through my body. We had done it. Our relationship was out in the open now.

Nick nodded slowly as he offered me his hand. "Okay. I'm keeping my eye on you," he said with a smile.

I smiled, shaking his hand. "Of course."

Rachel began to tell him something, and I looked down at Hannah. "Are you okay?"

She nodded. "I think I am. I'm sorry about my mom." She bit her lip. "I'm sorry about everything. You have been through so much for me, Nathan."

I smiled as I reached for her hand and squeezed it.

"You are so worth it."

CHAPTER 34

"So worth it."

I smiled at Nathan's words and then reached up and kissed him.

"I am out," I heard Nick say somewhere behind us.

When we pulled apart, Nathan and I were alone. That hadn't gone horribly wrong. I knew my mom wasn't going to be okay with our relationship. I wasn't ready for her reaction but at least it was over now. I could only hope she would get over it soon.

"Now that that's over." Nathan smiled shyly. "I wanted to ask you something."

"What?" I asked, looking up at him.

"It's Jared's birthday today and Jenni invited me over for a small party at their house. I wasn't going to go but," he shrugged, "I thought it would be a good time for you to meet them."

I smiled. "I would love to. It would be our first date."

"Of many more," he promised, leaning in to kiss me.

I pulled away after a moment. "Did my dad fire you?"

He shook his head. "He actually offered to promote me but I said no."

"Why?"

He touched my hair. "Because I am capable of finding a job on my own. I don't want to depend on your family."

He really was the whole package. I didn't know what I did to deserve him but I silently thanked God for putting him in my life.

"But you're still my bodyguard, right?" I wanted to make sure. I didn't want Nathan to stop being my bodyguard. I was so used to him by now. It was going to be hard when he did leave.

He chuckled. "Yes, ma'am."

I smiled, feeling happy that I would get to keep him at least until he found another job.

"Where are you going to work?" I asked him.

"When Jared and I came back from the military—"

"That's where you two met?" I interrupted. I realized I hardly knew anything about him. I yearned to learn every detail about him.

He nodded. "Yes. Anyway, we were offered a job as police officers. At the time, I had already started to work as a bodyguard so I declined it. Jared accepted it. I'm hoping he is able to help me get a job there."

"As a cop?" I smiled. He would make a really hot cop.

He nodded again. "Yes."

"Well, as your girlfriend, I support you."

He smiled as he shook his head. "You are amazing, you know that?"

"Thank you," I said, suddenly feeling a little shy.

"You are." He kissed my forehead. "Now, I should get back to work. I don't want your family to think I am taking advantage here."

I smiled. "You can take advantage of me any day."

He laughed. "I won't take those words for granted," he warned.

"Please don't," I joked, making him laugh again.

"Can we leave around six?" he asked.

I nodded. "Sounds good."

He ran a hand through his hair. "Okay. I'll get back to work now."

"Okay," I said, not moving.

He shook his head with a smile and then leaned in to kiss me before turning around and walking out. I stood in the middle of the living room for a moment.

As I made my way up the stairs, it felt like I was flying. I couldn't shake off the huge smile on my face. When I got to my room, I decided to do some homework since I had been procrastinating to the max. I was able to finish some of it and around five, I began to get ready. I did my hair first—just did some waves with the iron. The sound of my computer ringing made me stand up and walk across the room. I smiled as I answered the FaceTime call.

"What have I told you about Facetimes?" I told Patrick. "You need to make appointments for these types of things."

He laughed. "You're a dork." He was lying down, with the laptop on top of his chest. I could see that he was wearing a shirt, his hair was pulled back by a cap. It was good to see him. He had been here about three months ago, when I got out of the hospital. He stayed for about two weeks and I hadn't seen him since then. I placed the laptop on the edge of the bed, facing the closet.

"Where are you going?" he asked as he sat up, suddenly interested.

"Out." I smiled. "With Nathan."

"Wait—are you two official now?"

I smiled then told him about what had happened that day as he munched on chips on the other side.

"Make sure you send the wedding invitation when he proposes," Patrick said after I was done.

I rolled my eyes at him. "We just became official, Pat. Besides, I do want to graduate first."

"You're putting on jeans?" he asked in disbelief when he saw me putting them on.

"Yeah?" I asked.

"Hannah, take them off," he ordered, sounding annoyed.

I sighed but went into my closet and took them off.

185

"Take me in your closet!" I heard Patrick yell from the computer.

"No!" I said, laughing as I looked around my closet.

I changed into a black pencil skirt and a white button-down blouse.

Patrick frowned when he saw me. "Are you going to a party or a job interview?"

"Oh my god. It's not the kind of party you're thinking you know," I said as I went back to my closet and took off the clothes.

I put on a black dress that went down to my knees because you just couldn't go bad with black. The sleeves went down to my elbows then I put on my black high heels.

"Hey, you did have decent clothes somewhere in there," Patrick said when I walked out.

I rolled my eyes at him. "Wow, thanks."

He smiled. "You look hot. He's one lucky guy."

I smiled as I applied some mascara on my lashes. I was never really big on make-up—mostly because I didn't know how to use it. Girls went all out nowadays; everyone had turned into make-up artists. I also applied light make up on my eyebrows, just enough to fill them in.

"I have to go," I told Patrick as I reached for my purse.

"Okay," he winked. "Go get some."

I shook my head with a smile. "You're too much."

He laughed. "I'll call you later, Hannah Banana. Love you."

"Love you," I said then ended the call. I shut the laptop and then made my way out. I felt weird wearing high heels. I didn't use them very often but I wanted to make a good impression on Nathan's friends. I knew they were the closest thing he had to a family and it was important to me that they liked me.

The house was quiet when I reached the living room. I walked out the front door.

Outside was a car I hadn't seen before. It was a dark grey car. I didn't know what type it was because I knew nothing about cars other than that they needed gas to run, but it was beautiful. It looked brand new and Nathan was standing by it.

I frowned. "Is this your car?"

He nodded. "Yes."

"I didn't know you had a car."

He shrugged. "I don't use it much because I'm mostly always here but now I can use it to take you out." He smiled as his eyes roamed over my body. "You look wonderful."

I noticed that he was wearing a black suit with a white shirt and red tie. He offered me his hand. I took it and he opened the door for me. I watched as he walked around the car to the driver's side.

"So your friends..." I began as he drove.

"My friends..." he said when I didn't say anything.

"Do they know about me?"

"Yes," he answered slowly then frowned. "I need to tell you something."

I looked at him, not liking the tone of his voice. "Is it bad?"

He glanced at me for a second and then turned his attention back on the road. "Jenni has a friend...that I dated a few months back. It was really important for Jenni that Leah and I got together but I was never serious with her. I'm telling you because there is a chance Jenni may have invited her."

I nodded. I didn't like the idea of Nathan being with someone else at all. I found myself feeling a little angry, which was stupid because Nathan was with me now.

"Okay," I said.

He reached for my hand and held it against his lap. "There's nothing to worry about," he promised.

"Okay," I repeated.

The house was a twenty-five-minute drive from mine. It was in the suburbs. All the houses here looked the same: they were two story houses with windows everywhere and perfect lawns of green grass surrounded by beautiful green trees. Jared's house was white and pale pink. I loved their house.

"It's so beautiful," I said as we got out of the car.

Nathan put his arm around my waist, leaning me against the car. "You're beautiful," he said then frowned. "You know, on second thought, I'm not sure I want to go inside."

"Why not?" I asked.

"I just don't want to share you with anyone." He looked into my eyes and whispered, "I keep thinking of ways I could rip that dress off of you."

I blushed. "Nathan, stop it."

He chuckled then leaned in to kiss me. I put my hand behind his neck and pressed myself closer to him. I was wearing high heels so I reached up to his chin. I decided I should wear high heels more often. I kissed his neck right next to his Adam's apple, teasingly, making him sigh.

"You're not helping," he complained.

I laughed pushing him away gently. "You started it."

"True," he said as he reached for my hand. We walked to the front door.

Light was illuminating the windows and I could hear people laughing and talking inside.

I began to get a little nervous. It had been a while since I had been to a grown-up party and I was a little rusty in the social department.

"Here it goes," Nathan said as he reached for the doorknob and opened the door.

CHAPTER 35

The first thing I noticed about inside was that it was warm. The second thing was the smell of apple pie which made my mouth water. The third and scariest thing was the people.

There wasn't an exaggerated number of people but they were enough to make me even more nervous. Nathan had only talked about Jenni and Jared so I figured these people inside were all their friends and family. The living room was filled with people chatting while drinking wine. I could tell it was an adult party but there were still a few kids running around, bumping into everyone as they chased each other. Everyone seemed very outgoing, and they were all dressed very nicely. I realized that the pencil skirt and button-down blouse would have fit right in. I made a mental note to rub it in Patrick's face later.

"Nathan!" a man called as he put his hand on Nathan's shoulder.

Nathan smiled. "Hey, man," he said as they hugged. "Hannah, this is Jared," he said looking at me.

Jared was a very handsome black man. He was as tall as Nathan with broad shoulders and a muscular chest. He was wearing a red button-down shirt tucked into dressed black pants and black shiny shoes. He smiled at me, showing off his perfect white teeth. "Hey, Hannah, it's a pleasure to finally meet you." He shook my hand. "He wouldn't stop talking about you the last time he was here," he whispered.

Nathan rolled his eyes at him. "Wow, thanks man."

Jared chuckled and I smiled at him. "It's nice to meet you too."

"How's Jenni?" Nathan asked.

Jared raised an eyebrow. "Bigger."

"Hey! I heard that!"

Jenni was *really* pregnant. If I had to guess, I would say she was eight months pregnant. Her stomach was big and round. She was wearing an orange dress that complimented her dark skin, with her black hair around her shoulders. She was a beautiful woman. She and Jared looked great together. She hugged Nathan while I stood awkwardly to the side.

"That's Hannah!" Jared said to her looking at me.

"Oh!" Jenni said as she smiled at me. "Hi, I'm Jenni." She looked at Nathan apologetically. "I might have invited Leah. I'm sorry I didn't know you were coming."

I felt Nathan tensed a little next to me and I realized my body was a little tensed as well.

Relax, Hannah, relax.

"It's okay, Jenni. I'm here with Hannah," Nathan said, reaching for my hand again.

"Why don't we get you guys some food?" Jenni suggested. "Come on," she said then turned around.

"I watched your dad's movie by the way," Jared said as we followed Jenni to the dining room. "He was really good."

I smiled. "Thanks."

"Any chance I could meet him one day?" he asked.

"Jared, *what*—?" Nathan said with a frown.

I laughed. "It's okay," I smiled at Jared. "Sure, but I don't know when. He's leaving soon to start filming again."

"Is it a sequel to his last film?" Jared asked.

I frowned. "I know it's hard to believe this but I actually don't know. I don't really follow his movies that much. I try to avoid them."

"That's strange," Jared said, making me laugh.

We had reached the dining room and took a seat. I was glad Nathan didn't let go of my hand and kept it on his lap.

"Well, I already ate but I guess I'm going to have to join you guys," Jared shrugged.

I laughed. I am beginning to really like him. Jenni came over with a thin woman who helped her bring the plates. We were having meatloaf with mashed potatoes and gravy.

"Thank you," I said as she placed the plate in front of me. "It looks delicious."

Jenni placed her hand on my shoulders as she smiled. "You're welcome. You know I met your sister-in-law, Rachel, once?"

Jared chuckled. "Honey, we saw her across the room."

Jenni shook her head at him but she was laughing. "Okay, maybe I'm exaggerating."

I laughed. I really did like them. Our laugh was cut short by Leah. At least I guessed it was her by the way Nathan's hand tightened around mine.

Leah was tall and skinny with wild curly brown hair and big blue eyes. She was wearing a pencil dress that revealed her perfect long legs and high heels. She was wearing make-up and well, she was not ugly. I didn't know why but I got the feeling that I had seen her before. I knew Nathan had mentioned that she was a friend of Jenni.

"Nathan." She smiled at him and then walked around the table.

Nathan stood up and pulled me up with him. "Hello, Leah."

Leah completely ignored me. "How are you? Can I give you a hug?" she said, already opening her arms. Nathan put his free arm around her shoulders and hugged her awkwardly. "You look great," Leah said checking him out.

Nathan half-smiled then looked at me. "This is Leah," he told me. He was studying me close with his green eyes.

I nodded slowly as I looked at Leah who was finally acknowledging my existence. "Hello," I said, waving at her awkwardly with my fingers.

191

"Hannah Collins, right?" she said.

I nodded again. "Right."

She frowned with a smile. "I don't understand." She looked at Nathan. "Aren't you her bodyguard?"

Nathan nodded once. "I am."

Leah was either really super confused or she was being overdramatic. "Nathan, could we talk for a minute?" she asked.

Nathan hesitated.

"Come on, just a minute," Leah insisted. "I'm sure Jared can keep Hannah company."

Nathan looked at me with an apologetic look on his face.

I smiled at him. "It's okay."

It wasn't but I didn't want to look like a bitch in front of his friends. Frankly, I wanted to know what Leah wanted to talk to him about. Why had Nathan waited to tell me about her? I wished he would have been more honest with me.

He surprised me when he leaned in and pressed his lips on mine. "I'll be right back," he promised before walking away.

I was smiling, pretty satisfied, as I sat back down.

"Well, that was awkward," Jared said.

I laughed softly. "Yes, it was."

I picked up my fork and began to eat. Food was the only thing that comforted me when I was anxious.

"You have nothing to worry about," Jared assured me.

I smiled. "Thank you."

He looked at me and smiled. "He loves you, you know."

My chest warmed at his words. "I love him too."

"Good," Jared smiled. "I have never seen him like this. It's actually kind of annoying." He chuckled. "But I'm happy for him. Nathan deserves to be happy and there must be something really special about you that made him fall for you."

I smiled. "Thank you, Jared."

"Nathan told us you design wedding dresses," Jenni said as she sat next to Jared with a plate of apple pie.

"I like to draw, yes," I said slowly.

"Don't be modest," Jenni smiled.

I shrugged. "I'm still in school. I'll graduate next year. How far along are you?" I asked when I saw her placed her hands on her stomach.

"Eight." She smiled. "Three more weeks and we'll soon see her."

"Is she your first baby?" I asked as I crossed my legs. I was starting to relax a little.

"No." She smiled as she pointed at one of the little boys who were playing with some cars on the furniture. He was really cute in his little suit. "That little one is ours too."

"Well, you guys have a beautiful family," I said, smiling at them. I reached for my glass of wine and took a sip.

Jared nodded with a smile. "We are not as cool as your family but yes, I have to agree with you on that one," he said as he leaned in and kissed Jenni's forehead.

Jenni rolled her eyes. "He clearly admires your family."

I smiled. I was so used to people thinking that I had the perfect and best family in the world, that I had learned to keep my mouth shut. There was no need for me to tell them how imperfect my family really was. People were still going to think what the magazines portrayed. Besides, they were my family and I loved them regardless.

Nathan came back shortly and I felt my body relax as he took a seat next to me again and reached for my hand. He and Jared kept the conversation going by telling stories about their days back in the military. As it turned out, they weren't always the best of friends; they loved competing against each other too. Once in a while, Jenni would stand up, mingle with her guests and then she would come and sit with us again. Nathan and I ended up being the last ones to leave at around midnight.

"It was a pleasure to finally meet you, Hannah," Jared said as he surprised me with a hug.

"Okay, enough," Nathan said, pulling him away making him laugh.

"Thank you for having me," I smiled at them. "It was nice meeting you."

"My baby shower is next week, please do come," Jenni said.

I nodded. "Okay, thank you."

Nathan hugged them goodbye and then we both walked back to the car.

"They're really great," I said as he drove us back to the house.

He smiled. "Yes, they are."

I leaned my head on the headrest, suddenly feeling tired. I also felt really full, I had eaten more than I should have. Jenni had cooked some really delicious food.

"I'm sorry about Leah," Nathan said after a moment.

"It's okay."

"I would never do anything to hurt you, Hannah," he said, reaching for my hand again.

I turned and smiled at him. "I know."

The house was dark when we arrived. My dad still hadn't decreased the number of bodyguards that guarded our house which meant that he was still worrying. I wanted to tell him that it didn't matter how many bodyguards he hired, people would still find a way to hurt us if they wanted to which was scary to think about. Although things weren't as tense as they were a few months ago. Things were starting to go back to normal. But I couldn't blame my dad for being too careful.

"I'll see you tomorrow," Nathan said as we walked to the front door.

I smiled. "I can't wait."

He chuckled. "Me either." He put his arms around me. "I miss you already."

I kissed him. "I love you, Nathan."

He smiled against my lips. "I love you more."

I frowned. "Yeah, I don't think so."

He nodded. "I know I do. I can't live without you. You are mine." He kissed me. "I'm never going to let you go. You're stuck with me forever," he warned.

I laughed. "Good."

He kissed me one more time and then let me go. "Walk away before I drag you to my room."

"Very, very tempting," I said, smiling at him.

He chuckled. "Hannah, I'm warning you."

I laughed but turned around and began to unlock the door because I was really exhausted.

"Good night, love," Nathan said behind me.

I turned around and kissed him one more time. "Good night," I said against his lips and then turned around and walked in.

I was smiling all the way up to my room and as I took off the dress and shoes. I was smiling as I lay on my bed and closed my eyes. I fell asleep quickly and with a smile on my face.

CHAPTER 36

The next month went by really quick probably because of all the assignments I had due for school, considering it was the last month before summer. I was swamped with homework and being Nathan's girlfriend turned out to be very distracting, not that I minded.

I was Nathan's girlfriend.

My bodyguard was also my boyfriend. I didn't know why but there was something hot about the thought of dating your bodyguard. It was fulfilling. I loved it. I wanted him to be my bodyguard for the rest of my life, mostly because of all the time we spent together. Of course, I knew he wouldn't be my bodyguard for long which was why I wanted to enjoy it as much as possible.

Before I knew it, the month of April was gone and I was out of school. Now, I had three months of vacation. Three months to enjoy my boyfriend to the fullest.

Nathan was a great bodyguard but he was an even better boyfriend. He was perfect. Everything was unbelievably perfect. School was over. I had an amazing boyfriend. There wasn't any drama in my family…except for my mom.

She still hadn't accepted Nathan as my bodyguard and liked to remind me every chance she got. It saddened me because she was my mom and I loved her but I wasn't going to break up with Nathan just because she didn't like him. Nathan was my happiness and I wasn't going to give him up. I hoped my mom would get over it in time.

On a late afternoon in the middle of May, Nathan and I just got home when I saw my mom waiting for us outside by the front door.

"Hannah, I need to speak with you," she said, looking at me.

Before I could protest, Nathan nodded at me. "It's okay. I'll be in the kitchen," he said then let go of my hand and walked around the house.

"Come on, this is serious," my mom said as she walked into the house.

"Mom, what is going on?" I asked as she led me to my dad's office. She took a seat behind the desk and I sat down on the opposite side. She had a pale yellow document folder in front of her.

Somehow, I knew my perfect afternoon was about to get ruined. Nathan and I had gone out to celebrate his acceptance into the New York Police Department. His military background had qualified him. He had been interviewed about two weeks ago and they told him he was hired today. I was both happy and sad.

Happy because he was and I knew he wanted that job. I was sad because that I meant he wasn't going to be my bodyguard anymore so we weren't going to spend as much time together. I was going to have to find a job or something to do so the time wouldn't drag. I had become so used to being around him, it was going to suck when he started working. I knew that was selfish but I couldn't help it.

"I had Nathan investigated," my mom broke into my thoughts.

"What?" I asked, my eyes wide with disbelief.

She ignored my reaction and continued with her authoritative tone. "There was something about him that I knew he was lying about. And this—" she grabbed the folder, "—is proof."

"What is this?" I asked as I grabbed the folder. I opened it and inside were pictures—pictures of Nathan kissing another woman. I felt my heart began to accelerate as fear began to creep in.

"That's your beloved Nathan," my mom said. "That woman is Leah Lewis. She is a model. Nathan worked for her before I hired him."

I looked up at her. "I don't understand what you are insinuating, Mom."

Her stare was cold. "Don't be an idiot, Hannah. Don't you see? This is what he does! He sleeps with the women he 'protects,'" she said, her fingers mimicked an air quote.

I shook my head. "No, there has to be an explanation." I stood up. I grabbed the pictures and tried to turn around but my mom clasped her hand around my wrist, keeping me in place.

"Stop it!" She hissed at me. "Stop being an idiot! That man is not good for you, Hannah! Wake up!"

I stared at her in disbelief, tears began to fill my eyes. "Why are you doing this? Why are you hurting me?" I demanded, my voice breaking in the end.

She shook her head. "I'm keeping you from getting hurt, Hannah. Don't you see? I am doing this to spare you from heartbreak."

I shook my head angrily at her. "I'm sure there's an explanation to this, Mom. Why are you doing this to me? Why do you hate me so much?"

Her grip around my wrist loosened. "Oh, don't be ridiculous, Hannah. You're not a teenager anymore so stop acting like one. That man is no good for you. Stop being naïve. Open your eyes."

There was coldness in her voice that hurt me. She had always treated me differently. She never understood me. I couldn't believe I actually thought she had changed. I couldn't understand why she was like this. I wanted to curl up in a ball and cry but I swallowed the knot in my throat and looked at her.

"I love Nathan, Mom, and this—" I reached for the folder, "—has an explanation. I'll show you."

Without another word, I pulled my wrist free from her grasp and turned around.

198

"Don't come to me crying when he disappoints you!" she said behind me as I walked out of the office.

I stayed in the hallway for a moment, breathing hard. A million things were going through my head. I didn't understand my mom. The fact that she hired an investigator to investigate Nathan was just unbelievable. I didn't think she would go this far. I couldn't believe it. She had actually gone through all that trouble to make me break up with him. She couldn't understand that I loved him; she probably never would.

And then I thought about Nathan and that woman he was kissing in the picture. He had failed to mention that he was Leah's bodyguard. I shook my head and leaned against the wall.

No, it couldn't be true. Nathan wasn't a player. He was different. He had to be. I didn't want to overreact which was something the old Hannah would do. The old Hannah would overreact and start cursing guys and love. I wasn't like that anymore. Nathan had changed that.

I took a deep breath and began to walk down the hallway. I looked for Nathan in the kitchen and his room but he wasn't there. I found him outside, standing by one of the trees. I stood in the living room and watched him from the window.

He wasn't facing my way so I knew he couldn't see me. As I watched him, I thought about the past few weeks. I thought about every kiss, every touch, every look. It couldn't have been an act.

Just ask him, I thought to myself.

I clutched the folder onto my chest to hide my shaky hands as I made my way outside. It was dark outside. The sound of crickets filled the night. The lamps illuminated the garden. The number of bodyguards guarding the house had finally decreased and there were only a few shadows in the dark.

Nathan turned when he heard me approaching him. He smiled. "Hey."

"Hey," I stood in front of him, avoiding his gaze.

"What's wrong?" he asked as he studied me.

199

I finally looked up at him. I didn't say anything for a moment.

Nathan frowned. "Hannah, what's wrong?"

"How—" I cleared my throat, "—how did you meet Leah?"

"What?" He looked confused. "Why are you asking me that?"

"Just answer the question," I said. "And please be honest."

He clenched his jaw. "I was her bodyguard."

I closed my eyes as I nodded. "Were you sleeping with her too?" I asked looking at him.

"No, Hannah." He shook his head. "This is why I didn't tell you. I knew you were going to think that."

"It would have been better if you would have told me," I said. "Then I wouldn't have looked like an idiot in front of my mom."

"Your mom?" He frowned. "What does your mom have to do with this?"

I hesitated before handing him the folder. I watched as he took it and looked down at the pictures. "She had you investigated," I explained, looking away. "Said she did it to protect me."

Nathan looked at me in disbelief. "Hannah, please, believe me. These pictures were taken years ago by Leah. It was never like that with her. She was manipulative and liked to abuse her power. I put up with it because she was Jenni's friend until I couldn't," he said as he reached out and put his hands on my shoulder. "I'm sorry I didn't tell you the whole truth before. Please believe me when I tell you that whatever it was with Leah, it wasn't love. I love *you*, Hannah."

I looked at him for a moment. I knew he was saying the truth. I knew Nathan now and from the moment my mom showed me those pictures, I knew there was an explanation. I was just a bit hurt that Nathan hadn't told me the truth. "Anything else I should know?" I finally asked him.

200

"That night at Jared's house, she wanted to pretend that we were good friends," he said. "You see, I ended up quitting when she wouldn't stop harassing me. She wanted to act like none of it had happened. I wasn't going to have it so I just left her outside."

I nodded slowly. "Please don't hide things from me again."

"I promise I won't," he said.

I nodded again and then put my arms around him and buried my face in his chest. "I believe you," I whispered.

He tightened his arms around me in response and we stayed like that for the longest time.

CHAPTER 37

I bit my lip nervously as I looked out the window.

Today was the day. Nathan had met with Steve Powell. He had asked me to wait for him at my parent's house, so here I was with them and Nick and Rachel. Nathan had texted me a few minutes ago to let me know he was on his way. He was being so suspicious. I knew that what he had to say wasn't good news or else he wouldn't have asked me to gather everyone around.

I glanced at my mom. Her hands seemed a bit shaky as she poured herself a glass of wine. It had been a week and I was still angry at her for what she did. Getting Nathan investigated then trying to use that to sabotage my relationship with him had been a real low. I thought she had changed for good but maybe I was wrong.

"Why did Nathan asked us to meet him again?" Nick broke the silence in the living room.

They all turned to look at me. I didn't know what to say. I didn't know much myself. All I knew was that he was coming from his meeting with Steve Powell.

"Hannah?" my dad pressed.

"I don't know, Dad. I-I asked Nathan to go see Steve Powell for me in jail."

"Why did you do that? I thought you wanted nothing to do with him," Nick said.

"I didn't but I had questions and since I didn't want to go there myself, I asked Nathan to do it." I paused. "He met with him this afternoon and he just asked me to wait for him here with everyone."

"What?" my mom asked. "Are you both out of your mind?"

"Mom, I don't think it's that big of a deal," Nick said slowly. "I think it's fair that Hannah has questions she needs answered, and I think it was nice of Nathan to go for her."

"But what could you possibly want from that man?" my mom asked me. "He-he is a criminal! You should have just left things alone."

I played with the necklace I had in my pocket, wondering if this was a good time to bring it up. I wanted to know what Steve had to say about it before I told my mom that I had found it. She thought she had lost it. I'm sure she would be happy to know that I had found it since it was special to her. I remembered asking for it once when I was younger and she had refused to let me have it.

Before I could say anything, the doorbell rang and I rushed to the front door. Nathan had a look of dread on his face when I opened it.

"Hey," I said when he didn't say anything.

He put his arms around me and hugged me tightly.

"Nathan, what's wrong?"

He pulled away and offered me a sad smile. "Just promise me you'll be strong, okay?"

"You're scaring me."

"I know, I'm sorry." He reached for my hand. "Come on."

The tension back in the living room seem to have multiplied when Nathan and I joined everybody else. My dad took a step forward. He seemed impatient. "Nathan, please tell us what this is about."

Nathan nodded. "I went to speak with Steve and what he told me..." he looked around the room. "I thought it was important for everyone to be here."

"And what gave you the right to get in our business?" my mom demanded looking at Nathan angrily.

"Mom, I told you I asked him to go," I said with a frown. *Why was she acting like this?* "Please let Nathan speak."

203

"Nathan, please," Nick said with a nod, motioning Nathan to go on.

Nathan clenched his jaw. "Steve…he said… he told me why he did it."

"Stop it!" Mom interrupted. "Why are you all listening to him? He's a liar!"

"Christina!" Dad yelled. "That's enough!"

I wanted to cry. I hated arguments. I was so scared of what Nathan was going to say and I didn't even know why.

Mom looked taken aback by Dad's reaction so she finally shut up. My dad turned to look at Nathan. "Go on, Nathan, what did he tell you?"

Nathan looked uncomfortable. He focused on me as he spoke. "He told me that, uh, he hadn't done it alone. He said he—"

"Nathan, please just spit it out," Nick said impatiently.

Nathan looked at my dad. "He told me that he had a relationship with your wife, sir, and when she tried to end it, Steve blackmailed her. He'd expose their affair to you, and he said he told her to give him 2 million dollars in exchange, he would leave her alone. Your wife didn't have that money so Steve suggested that he'd take Hannah and get you to pay instead, as ransom."

"Oh, for God's sake!" my mom screamed. "He's lying! You can't possibly believe him! He's lying!"

My dad turned to look at her. "If he's lying, then why were you so scared that I go see that man?" He grabbed her by the shoulders. "Tell me the truth, Christina! Is this true? Did you know about Hannah's kidnapping before it happened?"

"No! Richard, please! You can't believe him!" Mom pointed at Nathan. "He's a liar!"

My dad shook her. "Christina, stop! Look at me! Is this true?"

I couldn't believe what was happening. *This couldn't be real, right? This had to be some kind of horrible nightmare.*

This nightmare is far from over, darling. Steve's words echoed in my head.

I reached for the gold necklace in my pocket. Then I walked up to my mom and raised the necklace in front of her.

"I found this in Steve's office the day we were rescued," I said, surprised by how steady my voice sounded. "You showed this to me a long time ago. It's the gold necklace you'd had since you were a teenager. I asked you then if I could have it and you said I couldn't because this was a very special necklace. It was your mom's."

My mom shook her head. "There could be many necklaces like that one!"

"You said you lost it," I said, ignoring her lame excuse. "When I asked you about the necklace, you said you lost it."

"No!" She was crying now. "No, that's not mine! That's not mine!"

"Christina!" Dad was shaking her. "Stop playing games and tell me the truth!"

"I told him not to do it!" My mother finally caved in. "I told Steve not do it!"

"*Oh, my god*," Rachel gasped behind me. I felt her put her hands on my shoulders.

"*Jesus Christ*," my dad exclaimed. "How could you do that? How could you do that to your own daughter?"

The house was filled with my mom's cries. "No," she cried. "I didn't do anything! I told him not to do it! I told him I would get the money through some other way. He blackmailed me! He said if I didn't give him the money, he would expose me! I didn't want to lose you, Richard!" She tried to touch my dad. "I didn't want to break our marriage!"

"Our marriage was broken the moment you cheated on me with that man!" my dad said as he pushed her to the ground.

"Dad!" Nick said as he hurried to help my mom off the ground.

"I can't believe this!" my dad screamed. "What kind of monster are you? He could have killed Hannah!"

205

"No." My mom shook her head. "He promised me he wasn't going to hurt her!"

"You knew about this." My dad shook his head in utter disbelief. "You knew about it and you didn't alert the police! You were more concerned about reputation than your daughter's wellbeing when this was all your own doing!"

My body was trembling but I was numb. I didn't feel anything. Everything was slowly making sense: why Steve promised me that he wasn't going to hurt me and why he had my mom's gold necklace. No wonder they easily got in the house despite the number of guards we had to secure the place. My mom probably helped them get in.

"Why?" I asked, looking at my mom. "Why, Mom? Didn't you ever love me?"

"I'm so sorry," she said. "I was scared. . He said he wouldn't hurt you! And he didn't, did he!"

"You let those men take me," I said, looking at her straight in the eye. I wanted her to know how angry I was. "You didn't care about me at all. The only thing you cared about was keeping your affair a secret."

"This is all your father's fault!" she surprising said, pointing at my dad. "You were gone all the time! I was lonely and needed to be loved, Richard! Steve was there when you weren't!"

"Don't you try to pin this on me, Christina," my dad told her. "If you weren't happy with me, you should have told me. You could have left and we would have gotten a divorce, but why didn't you? I know why. You didn't want to lose me because losing me would mean you'd lose the lifestyle that you very much love. All you care about is money and what the society thinks of you! You disgust me! I want to leave!"

Mom cried loudly. "No! Please!"

Dad took a few steps forward so he could look directly at her. "Do you really think I can be with you after what you did? I don't ever want to see you again, Christina. I don't want you anywhere near me. I'm done with you!" He glared at her for a moment before turned and walked out of the room followed by a loud banging of the front door.

"No," my mom cried into her hands. "No, please, no. Please," she looked at me and then got on her knees, "Please, Hannah, please forgive me. Please..."

I couldn't hold the tears any longer. They began to run down my cheeks as I looked down at my mom. "Stop, Mom, get on your feet," I said, reaching down. I grabbed her by the arms and pulled her up. "Why did you do that? Do you have any idea what I am feeling right now? You have broken my heart," I said, my voice broke at the end.

"I'm sorry," she said, reaching out to wipe my tears with her hand. "I love you, you're my daughter. Please, Hannah, I asked Steve not to do it but he wouldn't listen! I thought I loved him but he turned out to be a completely different man! I didn't mean to hurt you! Please! You have to forgive me!" She put her hands on my shoulders.

"Oh, Mom," I said in disbelief. "

There were so many things I wanted to tell her but I couldn't. The knot in my throat could barely let me speak. "I'm sorryI can't." I shook my head then turned around and made my way out of the house.

I thought I was alone when I got outside but when I turned around, Nathan was there.

"I'm so sorry to have caused you this pain, Hannah," he said with a hurt expression on his face.

I shook my head as I cried. He put his arms around me and held me tightly as I tried to wrap my mind around the fact that my own mother had something to do with my kidnapping.

CHAPTER 38

I stared at the TV. screen in front of me. I was looking at it but I wasn't really watching it. My mind was a thousand miles away.

I let my head rest on Nathan's left thigh; I was stretched out on the couch. His hand was on my waist, stroking it in a soothing way. My mind kept going back to what had happened earlier in the day. It didn't feel real. It felt like someone else's life and I was only there watching it. It all felt almost like a movie.

I didn't think my mind could accept the fact that my own mother had known about the kidnapping before it happened and had done nothing to stop it.

I was kidnapped by her lover for money. I also thought about her relationship with Steve. According to Steve, it had started two years ago. I still didn't know how they met, but it didn't really matter. I could only imagine them meeting secretly in hotel rooms. I could only imagine how my mom gave Steve her gold necklace as a sign of her love for him.

But why did Mom decide to break off their relationship? My guess would be because Steve wanted more. Perhaps he wanted to go public but my mom didn't. But my mom couldn't give up her title as Richard Collins' wife. Steve was a simple salesman so he obviously didn't have the millions that my dad had. Clearly, my mom tried to break off their relationship and Steve refused, he probably harassed her for some time before he finally accepted the fact that they weren't going to be lovers anymore. It wasn't real love after all, but he wasn't going to let her go just like that.

Steve knew my dad had money so he blackmailed my mom and tried to extort $ 2 million from her by telling her he would only leave her alone if she would pay her the amount; he threatened to expose their affair if she refused.

I could only imagine how my mom became desperate. *How was she supposed to come up with 2 million dollars?* She couldn't just write a check of that amount without being questioned by my dad. There was no way for her to take that money from him without him noticing. Nathan told me that she tried to reason with Steve by asking for time but he refused. Steve came up an idea to kidnap me for ransom. He was convinced that my dad would pay that amount of money for his only daughter.

My mom tried to sabotage my relationship with Nathan yesterday and today I found out that she had known that Steve was trying to kidnap me and she didn't do anything to prevent it. She probably thought it was convenient to let Steve take me so my dad could pay the 2 million dollars as ransom and she would just wash her hands from the affair. If Steve hadn't talked, she could have gotten away with it. No one would had ever found out that she had been cheating on her husband for the past two years or that she had been behind my kidnapping. She was partly at fault for the killings in Miami. Nothing she could do would surprise me anymore.

My own mom…

This nightmare is far from over, darling.

Steve knew. He knew how this secret would break my family.

As I looked back on what happened, I didn't even realize that I was already crying until Nathan leaned forward to look at me.

"Oh, Hannah, come here," he said as he helped me sit up so he could put his arm around me. I buried my face in his chest; it was starting to feel like home there. "I'm so sorry, love," he murmured onto my hair.

I didn't know what I would have done if I didn't have Nathan with me. He was the one who gave me the protection and care that my heart needed. My heart was broken again, but unlike before, it was a guy who broke my heart this time, it was broken by my own flesh and blood—my mother.

How could I possibly move on from this? How could I keep going after knowing what my mother did?

"I'm here for you, Hannah," Nathan said softly. "I know I can't instantly take the pain away from you —I would if I could— but it's going to get better, babe. I promise it will."

I just nodded onto his chest so he knew that I appreciated his words, that I appreciated *him* more than he realized.

The only good thing about everything that happened was that it had brought me closer to Nathan. That was the only silver lining.

~

It was a Wednesday afternoon, about three weeks after we had found out the truth about my mom; she had moved out that same day. I knew Nick knew where she was and how she was doing, and I knew I would ask him someday about Mom, but not right now. I didn't want to know anything about her at the moment. Colton and Derek had both reached out to me in the past weeks. I had spent the day with Colton yesterday and with my dad the day before that. I had never spent more time with my family than now. I appreciated their support and it helped me but I knew that time was going to be the best healer for me.

I looked at the walls of the house. They were familiar but at the same time they felt foreign to me. This wasn't home anymore.

"You should buy a house," I said to Nick who was going through something on his laptop. "You should buy a house, take Rachel, and start growing your family."

Nathan had started working for NYPD a week ago. He thought about postponing his start date and I knew he wanted to do it because he was worried about me so I had to pick myself up for him. I didn't want him to put his career on hold for me. I was fine. I knew I was going to be okay.

Nick looked up at me curiously.

"I'm being serious, Nick," I said when he didn't say anything. "Don't you think Rachel deserves her own house? It's time."

Rachel wasn't at home. She was at work, organizing everything for her fashion show in two weeks. She was always the busiest during the weeks before her fashion event.

"Of course, she deserves it," Nick said. "It's just funny how apt it is that you mention it's time to grow my family when…"

I open my mouth. "What?"

He grinned. "We're having a baby."

"Really?"

He nodded. "She found out a few weeks ago. We didn't—it didn't seem appropriate to celebrate after…"

"Oh my god!" I exclaimed and stood up and went to give him a hug. "Are you kidding? You guys should have told me! Congratulations, Nick," I said as I hugged him.

He soon realized I was crying. "I'm sorry. I shouldn't have said anything—"

I shook my head as I pulled away. "No, these are happy tears," I said. "We are going to be okay. I'm going to be okay."

Nick put his hand on my shoulder. "I'm so sorry, Hannah. I know that what happened has hurt you so much. And I'm sorry if it seemed that I was defending her—"

"Stop, no," I sniffed. "What she did was horrible, but she is still our mom. I know I'm going to forgive her…eventually. Time heals all wounds." I half-smiled, trying to show him my optimism.

"You have grown so much, Hannah. When did that happen?"

"I have no idea," I admitted.

"Does Nathan have something to do with it?" he asked with a smile.

"He does. Definitely." I couldn't help but smile. "He makes me very happy."

"I'm glad," Nick said. "After everything that's happened, you deserve it."

"Thank you, Nickelodeon." I paused. "Don't think I've forgotten that you and I have a pending conversation."

"Pending conversation?" he frowned. "Oh," he said in realization.

"Nathan's conversation with Steve served as a confession to my kidnapping and what happened in Miami but he denied shooting you." I looked at him. "And it doesn't make sense for him to deny it if he was the one to do it. He was already in deep trouble."

Nick shifted uncomfortably in his chair. "Hannah…"

"You know who shot you, don't you?" I whispered. I was pretty sure it was just us in the house besides the service employees but they were probably downstairs.

His blue eyes met mine. It took him a moment to answer. "Yes."

"And you knew Steve wasn't behind it all this time?"

"Yes," he said looking ashamed. "I'm sorry. I felt bad about keeping that to myself and making you all believe it was all connected but I knew my silence wouldn't hurt anyone. This is just a secret I have to keep."

I frowned in confusion. "You know the shooter." I guessed. What else could it be? If Nick knew who shot him and he was willing to keep it a secret then it had to be because he knew the shooter and didn't want to turn them in.

"The less you know, the better."

I began to shake my head. "Nick—"

"Don't worry about me, Hannah. I'm an adult. I know what I'm doing. I'm just asking you to please keep this between us."

We looked at each other for a moment. I wanted to know what was up with him. I wanted to know what he knew but I also had to respect his privacy. Besides, he was right. He was an adult. I didn't understand it but he did. I knew he wouldn't hide anything that could potentially hurt Rachel or anyone else.

So I nodded. "Okay."

"Thank you." He chuckled nervously, easing the tension. "Now, you have to help me choose the perfect gift for Rachel. You actually gave me an idea."

I smiled. "I would love to. What are you thinking?"

A house. Nick wanted to get a house for Rachel. It was the perfect gift at the perfect time. We spent the rest of the afternoon checking houses around the area. I took note of the ones that we liked while Nick tried to contact the realtor. I felt excited again. I loved looking at houses. She was going to love her gift. I would make sure of that.

Rachel got home in the evening and I waited anxiously by the window. When I saw her car pull up, I hurried downstairs and opened the front door. She was just getting out of her car.

"Hannah?" she asked when she saw me walk out. "Is everything alright?"

"Uh, no, actually," I said as I walked down the porch steps. "I can't believe you didn't tell me you are pregnant."

She opened her mouth in surprise then shook her head with a smile. "Nick told you?"

"Yes." I smiled as I hugged her. "Congrats, Rachel. I am so happy for you and Nick. I cannot wait to be an aunt!"

She laughed as I pulled away. "I'm sorry we didn't tell you. It's just that with everything going on—"

"But this is good news!" I said. "This baby will bring happiness into our family."

"Aw, Hannah, you're gonna make me cry."

I smiled as I hugged her again. "This is so exciting, Rachel! Are you being careful with all the tedious preparations for the show? Maybe I can help you," I said, looking at her.

"Oh! Would you? You would be a great help! I have so many things to do and I've tried to not think about it so not stress myself more but that only adds more stress!"

We were walking up the stairs by now, reaching the front door.

"Of course, I would. I have nothing better to do," I said. Between helping her prepare for her show and helping Nick look for a house, I knew that would be enough to keep me busy for the next few weeks. I needed to get my mind busy. I had stopped

213

sketching for the moment due to lack of inspiration. This would be good as a distraction.

Moments after Rachel and I walked into the house, my dad arrived. Rachel told him the good news after greeting him which made my dad's face brighten as he smiled.

His brown eyes widened. "No way. Is that true Rachel?" Rachel nodded and he chuckled. "Oh! My first grandchild!"As he hugged and congratulated Rachel, my smile faded a little. My mom should have been here. I'm sure Nick was going to tell her about the baby, if he hadn't told her already. She should have shared this good news with us; the new addition to our family. It was just sad to realize why she wasn't with celebrating with us. I knew it would take some time before everyone of us could finally move on, but the worst had passed and it was the only that mattered. The nightmare was over and I knew it would only get better from here.

That night, Nathan sent me a text saying he was outside of my house. I was already in bed but I wasn't really sleepy. I had missed him all day. I hated the fact that he wasn't my bodyguard anymore but I knew that this was a huge step for us. We had a normal relationship now.

My dad had completely changed the security at home. He had enforced the home security and let the bodyguards go. He still had Robin but only when he had to be out in public Also, I finally felt like a normal person when my dad thought that it was no longer necessary for me to have my own bodyguard. It was crazy to think about how everything had changed in my life—for the better.

"Hey," I whispered to Nathan when I got outside.

He was leaning against his car, wearing his navy blue pants and white T-shirt under his uniform shirt. He looked so good in a uniform. He opened his arms for me and hugged me tightly. "I missed you," he whispered in my ear.

"I know, me too," I said as I pulled away to look at his handsome face. I put my hands around his neck.

"You look different," he noted.

I smiled. "Today was a good day. Rachel is pregnant."

He raised his eyebrows. "Really? Wow, that's awesome."

"I know. I'm so excited to be an aunt. I'm going to spoil that little baby."

Nathan chuckled. "Well, I'm glad that you had a good day."

I smiled as I touched his cheek with my palm. "You don't have to worry about me anymore. I'm going to be okay."

He smiled. "I'm always going to worry about you, Hannah. You're my everything."

I reached up and pressed my lips to his. "I hate that you're no longer my bodyguard."

He chuckled. "We could still role play you know..."

I laughed. "And you can call *me* naughty things."

He kissed me. "Mmm," he hummed against my lips. "I hate that I have to work tomorrow. I have a Friday off though."

"Good. I'm going to be busy too anyway. I'm going to help Rachel with her show and I'm also helping Nick look for a house."

"They're moving out?"

I nodded. "I sort of told him that they should. They're married. They should have been living in their own house from the beginning."

He looked at me, a glint of amusement in his green eyes. "So, we'd have to be married in order for you to move in with me?"

"Hmm...not necessarily..." I couldn't hide my smile.

"I wouldn't mind at all, anyway." He put both of his hands on my cheeks. "You are going to be my wife someday, Collins," he said in that playful voice, which reminded me of how we flirted with each other on our ride to Miami.

I looked into his eyes. "Do you mean that?"

"Absolutely," he said immediately. "I knew from the moment I saw you sitting under that tree that I was going to love you and make you my wife."

I rolled my eyes. "Sure, you did."

"I did," he said. "I love you, Hannah."

"I love *you*, Nathan." I smiled as he leaned in to kiss me.

"You will be my wife," he said against my lips.

215

"Sounds like a promise." I smiled.

He looked into my eyes and I could see it—I could see how much he loved me. This amazing man really did love me. There was no doubt in my mind, and I loved him. His lips curved into a crooked smile and then he whispered, "It is."

CHAPTER 39

The room was filled with lights everywhere. I was surrounded by people, holding their glasses of wine. Servers walked around with a tray, offering drinks to everyone. And I stood there, waiting anxiously for the show to begin.

It was late July and today was Rachel's big night. I had spent the last three weeks helping her and Nick, which turned out to be harder than I thought considering I couldn't tell Rachel anything about Nick's plan.

We had found the perfect house, and I couldn't wait for Rachel to see it. I knew she was going to be so happy about it. Nick and I had bought the furniture. While Rachel and I were busy for the event, Nick had moved her clothes to the new house. He had planned to surprise her with the house after the show.

As for my dad, we had come to that decision together to sell our own house. It didn't make sense to live in that massive house anymore when there were only just him and me now. I knew he was still worried about me and I didn't know what to do anymore to convince him that I was fine. The days after we found out the truth, he had sulked around, screaming at people on the phone. He was taking out his anger out on strangers. I told him how I had made myself busy for the past few weeks and how it had done me good. Thankfully, he had gotten better; he wasn't as angry anymore.

"Drink?"

I turned to look at the server who suddenly came up to me. He was tall with short, curly black hair and a nice trimmed beard. He was wearing a suit and he was offering me a glass of wine.

I took a step back. "Uh—"

Nathan had finally returned, holding two glasses of wine. He looked really good in his suit. He had put on a black vest on top of his white shirt today. I didn't think that I would ever *not* be impressed by how good-looking he was. He looked good in everything. I thought I looked like a potato next to him but Nathan always made me feel more beautiful than I probably was.

He had been working at NYPD for a few weeks now. I could tell that he really liked his job. I knew he would be great at it. It just hadn't occurred to me that he would continue to risk his life for other people. I knew that the risk was always a part of the job, but I just couldn't help but worry about him.

Nathan handed me a glass as he glared at the guy who suddenly looked really small next to him. "Get lost, mate."

The guy nodded once and then walked away.

Nathan looked at me. "I leave you alone for one minute," he said, shaking his head with a smile.

Nick suddenly joined us with a smile on his handsome face. "It's about to start," he said, raising his eyebrows, excitedly.

Sure enough, everyone began taking their seats. Nick, Nathan, and I were in the first row. I searched the room, looking for my brother, Colton, and found him sitting to our right, next to his colleague. He had come after all.

Everyone clapped as Rachel walked out wearing a beautiful long blue dress that fit her perfectly. Her long straight hair was up in a high ponytail. It was crazy to think how she had a tiny baby inside her. She gave her speech. I remembered back when she gave her first speech ever, she was so nervous then. I had seen her shake from where I was sitting, but now she was a natural. She knew what she was doing.

I crossed my legs in front of me as the show began. Nathan put his arm around my shoulders, trailing my arm with his fingers throughout the show.

As I watched Rachel's collection come to life, I thought about the day I could see my dresses come to life too. I still had a year of school left but it was so close I could almost taste it. I wanted to start working on it already, watching her collection gave me motivation and inspiration. I planned to have a boutique in the future—a future I couldn't wait for. I felt like I could do anything with Nathan next to me. As long as he was with me, I knew I was going to be happy.

After the show, we went with Nick and Rachel to celebrate at a restaurant Nick had booked exclusively for us. I liked the privacy.. Lately, we had begun to have a lot of double dates with them. It had started to become a thing.

"The show was amazing," I told Rachel over dinner.

Her face flushed. I knew for a fact that it was because she had cried. She smiled as she sighed. "I'm glad it's over. It's always so stressful. I don't think I could get used to it."

"I'm glad it's over too," Nick said. "Now you can give your undivided attention to your husband," he teased, looking at her. Rachel laughed and told him something.

I turned to look at Nathan who was looking at me. "You look beautiful," he whispered.

"You always say that," I said with a smile.

His green eyes looked mesmerizing. "Because you always do." He smiled.

"Hannah," Rachel called my name. I turned to look at her. "Can you believe that this guy wants me to have twins?"

I raised my eyebrows as I turned to look at Nick. "Oh yeah, easy for you to say since you're not the one who's gonna give birth to them."

"Exactly!" Rachel said.

We all laughed.

"I promise I'll help you with one of them," Nick said.

Rachel rolled her eyes at him. "Sure, you will. I mean, if they're twins great, but if not then it's still great."

Nick smiled. "I agree."

We talked some more as we finished dinner. It was a really good night. I loved the way Nathan showed his affection by holding my hand. Or putting his hand on my thigh. Or his arm around my shoulders. He did it so naturally, I was pretty sure I was the only one who noticed it.

After dessert, Nick stood up. "We're leaving, love birds."

"But we literally just finished eating. I'm stuffed," Rachel said as she leaned back on the chair.

"I have a surprise for you," Nick said, winking at her.

Rachel smiled. "Really? What is it?"

"Let's go so you can find out."

She sighed but she stood up then leaned in to hug me. "Thank you for coming."

"Always." I smiled at her. She waved at Nathan and then grabbed Nick's hand as they walked out together.

I reached for my martini and took a sip. I had been drinking way too much today. Suddenly, I felt Nathan's hands on my thighs and he spun me on the chair so that I was facing him.

"Nathan, *not here*," I whispered. The server was nowhere in sight but I knew he could come back any minute.

He chuckled. "Don't worry, I'll wait," he said, winking at me.

I shook my head with a smile.

"Move in with me," he suddenly said.

"What?" I asked, looking at him.

"Move in with me," he repeated. "If you want, we could get married first—"

"You would marry me?" I asked, with a flattered smile. I knew we had already talked about this but it was always flattering to hear him say it with so much confidence. I knew he really meant it.

"Of course, I would." He smiled. "I would have asked you already but I knew it was a bit too soon and I know you want to graduate first but—*I can't wait.*"

I laughed. "You're being serious?"

"Of course," he said. "I miss you when I'm not with you. I want to be with you every second of the day. I want to go to sleep with you next to me and I want to wake up with you. Hannah, I am

220

being serious. I love you and there is no doubt in my mind that I want to be with you forever so why wait?" he said as he took out a small box from his jacket.

"Nathan what—" my heart was beating hard against my chest.

"Don't freak out." He smiled. "I just happened to be around a jewelry store the other day and I ended up buying the ring."

"Oh, so it was super random," I teased.

"Totally random." He chuckled and then opened the box. A perfect one diamond ring stared back at me. "I know it's only been a few months since we began our relationship so I would understand if you don't want to get married right away, but I want you to move in with me. And this ring—" he took out the ring with his two fingers, "—is my promise to marry you when you're ready."

I was speechless for a moment. All I could do was stare into his green eyes.

"Are you proposing?" I finally asked.

"I'm sorry—" he said as he got down on one knee and took my left hand in his. "Hannah Collins, I know we are young; I know it might be too fast; I know I am not a millionaire; I know it's a little crazy, but I am crazy *about you*. I love you more than I love anything in this world. So, will you accept this ring as a promise to marry me whenever you are ready and would you give me the pleasure of moving in with me?"

I smiled. "Yes, of course!"

"Really?" he asked, looking a little surprised.

"Yes!" I said.

"Great!" He put the ring on my fourth finger. He stood up and wrapped his arms around my waist, pulling me up with him.

"It's so beautiful, Nathan, thank you so much," I said as I looked at the ring around my finger. It fit perfectly.

"I love you," he simply said as he leaned in to kiss me.

He bit my lower lip as we pulled away. He asked for a bottle of champagne when the server came to check on us. I laughed as he struggled to open the bottle.

It finally opened with a loud *pop!*

"We can get married and move in together," I said after we took the first sips. "I would love to do that. We can live together while our careers take off." Moving in with Nathan meant that my dad wouldn't have to worry about me anymore. It was the perfect solution for me and I couldn't wait to live with him.

He grinned. "You are a dream come true."

I laughed because that's what I had been saying about him. "I love you, Nathan."

His arm went around my waist. "I love you more, my Hannah." He leaned in to kiss me before I could protest. "I can't wait to make babies with you," he whispered with a teasing smile.

I laughed. "Yeah, that's going to be fun."

I couldn't wait to see how our kids would look like. I hoped they would look like Nathan. But most importantly, I hoped they were more like him. I hoped they would have his personality. I hoped they would know how to love like their dad.

But it wouldn't be until a few more years. Meanwhile, we could get married and live together. I suddenly couldn't wait for the moment to finally happen.

Nathan put his arms around me and pressed me closer to him. I listened to his heartbeat as we stood in silence. He pressed his lips against my forehead as he ran his hand through my hair.

"My Hannah," he whispered and I closed my eyes as I smiled. "My beautiful Hannah."

I was his and he was mine.

For as long as we could live.

Mine.

My Nathan.

My perfect Nathan.

My Possessive Bodyguard.

EPILOGUE

NATHAN

Today was the day.

I was wearing a gray suit with a white button-down shirt, gray vest, and a red tie…a small flower pinned on the right side of my jacket. I sighed nervously as I ran a hand through my hair for the hundredth time.

"Nathan."

I turned to look at Jared who was wearing a gray suit.

"It's time, man," he said with a smile. "Are you alright?"

I took a deep breath. "I'm a little nervous," I admitted.

"Don't worry, they'll be looking at her and not at you." He grinned.

That made me smile.

Hannah.

She was about to become my wife.

Finally.

It had been a long year. It had been a year since I gave her the ring. A year since we moved in together. I had never been so impatient in my life. I couldn't wait for this day. I hadn't slept last night just thinking about this day. Now, I couldn't wait until it was finally over. We had been living together but now I could actually call her my wife.

My wife.

We had moved into our new house over the weekend before our wedding. Hannah had graduated from school, and I had two weeks of vacation so we didn't have to worry about anything. It would just be the two of us.

223

I followed Jared out the door.

The wedding was taking place in a beautiful garden far from the city. It was a small wedding, only our closest friends and family were invited. But I didn't really care who would come as long as Hannah were here. I didn't need anyone else to marry her. Maybe, except for the judge. Chairs were lined up in rows and everyone was already here.

As I stood in front, at the altar, I looked around nervously.

It was happening.

It was finally happening.

I could see Nick, Colton, and Derek all seated on the front row. Nick was holding his three-month old son in his arms. Rachel was the maid of honor so she was with Hannah. I could see Jenni seated with her kids. She smiled at me when she saw me looking at her. Christina had been invited to the wedding, and she was sitting next to Derek quietly. Hannah had forgiven her, of course, but they were still working on patching up their relationship.

I began to move my leg, impatiently.

The altar was an arch made of beautiful white roses and the judge was standing behind it, looking at all of us. It wasn't a church wedding and I didn't really care. As long as we got married and Hannah could legally be called my wife.

As long as she was mine...

"It's time." Jared smiled as he stood next to me.

I could feel my heart beating hard against my chest as the orchestra began playing the song and everyone stood up. Rachel walked down the aisle first; she was wearing long a lavender dress. She smiled at me. The knot in my throat tightened when I saw her.

Hannah had designed her own dress. Her wedding dress was the first dress she had designed. It was a beautiful V-neck lace dress with sleeves down to her elbow. The cleavage was perfect and sexy. The dress fitted around her body, showing off her perfect hourglass shape, and it spread wider when it reached her knees. It had a small tail trailing behind her. She had a long veil covering her face and she was holding a flower bouquet.

224

She looked absolutely stunning. She looked sexy. She looked beautiful…and she was mine.

I found myself choked up and I wiped the tear that had rolled down my cheek as my *dream* began to walk down the aisle. Jared placed his hand on my shoulder and squeezed it.

Hannah and Richard finally reached me and I took Hannah's hand.

"She's yours now, Nathan," Richard said when we hugged. "Take care of her."

I was afraid I would break down crying if I spoke so I just nodded.

"You look…" I searched for the word. Beautiful was no longer enough. I shook my head. There were no words to describe how amazingly beautiful she looked.

She smiled at me. "Thank you."

The music had stopped and we were now supposed to be facing the judge. Problem was I couldn't take my eyes off of her which made her laugh when the judge was talking to me and I didn't even notice.

"Nathan," she whispered.

"Yes," I answered, making her laugh.

She was so amazing. I couldn't believe I was marrying the beauty in front of me.

The ceremony continued on. Jared and Rachel signed as witnesses and then Hannah and me. Hannah said her vows and by the time it was my turn to say my vows—I was at a loss for words.

"Hannah," I smiled as I looked at her. "*My* Hannah. I am so lucky to be here. I am so lucky to be by your side. You are everything I want. I love you more than life itself. You have changed my life." I stopped, trying to swallow the knot in my throat. "I promise to love you with every breath that I take. I promise to be by your side here and in Pluto," Hannah laughed but I could see the tears running down her cheeks, "I feel so—*happy* just by being around you. You are my sunshine. You make my world colorful. I love you. I love you very much and I promise to make you the happiest you can be for the rest of my life. This is forever."

People clapped as I put the wedding ring on her fourth finger.

"Now that Nathan and Hannah have given themselves to each other by solemn vows, with the joining of hands and the giving and receiving of rings, I pronounce them husband and wife!"

I pulled Hannah's veil over her head, revealing her beautiful porcelain face and pressed my lips against hers. I had to remind myself that her family and people were watching us. I couldn't wait to rip that dress off of her.

"I love you," I told her as everyone clapped around us. I wiped her tears with my thumb.

"I love *you*," she said as she smiled.

I grabbed her hand and together we walked down the aisle as *husband and wife*.

BOOK YOU MIGHT ENJOY

LIES, BETRAYAL & LOVE
Melissa Bender

People meet for a reason. No matter what anyone says, it's always for a reason. Oliver and Sage, two people who have never met before, shared an instant connection. A spark forms and a night neither of them will forget happened... Sage, a bubbly college student, remembers it from the bruises he left her. Oliver, a married guy, remembers it as a betrayal to his wife. Neither thinks they will see each other again. They move on with their lives and put that night behind them, but in an unexpected turn of events, they run into each other again. Emotions resurface and a secret that is much bigger than the two of them is about to be revealed. A secret that will hold them close together for the future to come. As the lies unravel, a horrible betrayal is unveiled to all, hurting those closest to them while a love like no other has already begun to bloom.

BOOK YOU MIGHT ENJOY

AMARA ROSE

HIS EX-WIFE
Amara Rose

Rafael Luciano, the love of my life; a sweet, handsome, amazing guy who's got me wrapped around his fingers, has pushed me out of his life. Life has been great and we are well on our way to having our first child. But one accursed day, he slams me with divorce papers and accuses me of being a gold-digger. Confused and heartbroken, I sign and leave. With a snap of a finger, everything is gone: my love, my life, and the father of my unborn child. How am I to get through all this? Will I be able to provide my daughter the life she deserves? Most importantly, what happened that day that made my sweet Rafael into a heartless monster?

ACKNOWLEDGEMENTS

My passion for writing began to grow from my passion for reading. I've always loved romance, and I began writing in notebooks when I was twelve years old. I still have most of the notebooks in a box somewhere in my room. I love going back and reading the stories I wrote through middle school then high school and, eventually, college.

I joined Wattpad in October 15, 2012. I never imagined the amount of readers or followers I would reach one day. I want to give a special thank you to all of my Wattpad readers. I wouldn't be where I am without them. All of you made it possible for me to hold this book in my hands. From the bottom of my heart, thank you.

I would also like to thank my family: my mom, my sister (Diane), and my brother (Yeiman). They didn't know how serious I was about writing up to a few months ago, but they have expressed support for me doing what I love. In fact, people that know me don't really know that I'm a writer. I've always seen writing as my safe haven, so it's something I kept to myself for a long time. I am now grateful to be able to speak about it freely and feel a sense of pride in doing so.

Finally, I want to thank God because it is His grace and love that have made this and everything else in my life possible.

Thank you all.

AUTHOR'S NOTE

Thank you so much for reading *My Possessive Bodyguard*! I can't express how grateful I am for reading something that was once just a thought inside my head.

Please feel free to send me an email. Just know that my publisher filters these emails. Good news is always welcome.
jamilexis_gallardo@awesomeauthors.org

Sign up for my blog for updates and freebies!
jamilexis-gallardo.awesomeauthors.org

One last thing: I'd love to hear your thoughts on the book. Please leave a review on Amazon or Goodreads because I just love reading your comments and getting to know you!

Can't wait to hear from you!

Jamilexis Gallardo

ABOUT THE AUTHOR

Jamilexis is a graduate from Arizona State University. She lives in Phoenix, Arizona, with her family. She writes in her free time (sometimes even at work) and spends time with her family and friends as well. *My Possessive Bodyguard* was originally published on Wattpad, along with other stories she has written over the years.

Made in the USA
San Bernardino, CA
08 September 2019